Funeral Expenses

Also by Pauline Bell

The Dead Do Not Praise
Feast Into Mourning
No Pleasure in Death
The Way of a Serpent
Downhill to Death
Sleeping Partners
A Multitude of Sins
Blood Ties
Stalker
Reasonable Death
Swansong
Nothing but the Truth

FUNERAL EXPENSES

Pauline Bell

Constable • London

Constable & Robinson Ltd
3 The Lanchesters
162 Fulham Palace Road
London W6 9ER
www.constablerobinson.com

First published in the UK by Constable,
an imprint of Constable & Robinson Ltd 2006

ISBN 13: 978-1-84529-223-2
ISBN 10: 1-84529-223-5

Printed and bound in the EU

For my friend and mentor
Norman Brown

Prologue

Prologue

By a happy coincidence, the largest florist shop in the town of Cloughton in West Yorkshire was owned by a man named Adam Flowers. He considered the Astramax the most suitable of modern runabout vans for his company's purposes. He was not happy, however, with any of the colours, red, white or blue, in which Vauxhall supplied them, and the small garage round the corner from the shop had a contract to spray three new vans each year in a fetching shade of leaf green. Mr Flowers thought this a more fitting background for the garland motif that surrounded his logo, written on the side of his vans in flowing script: 'Let Flowers Brighten Your Life!'

The owner's opinion of the vehicles was not shared by his drivers. One in particular always raked the street with his eyes lest any of his mates should observe him climbing in. Just now, however, he had other things on his mind.

Today he had misjudged the timing of the job. Because of the wealth of choice offered to him he had taken too long to make up his mind. Still, he'd got away just in time with his careful – too careful – selection of goods safely stowed away in one of the garishly decorated flower boxes stacked behind his seat. Now he had two sets of legitimately filled boxes still to deliver and twenty-five minutes to be back at base.

He'd deal with the smaller delivery first. Three boxes of white lilies and two of red carnations to St Thomas's where Doreen would be waiting to arrange them before she knocked off for the day. That funeral was for nine tomor-

7

row morning. To him, it seemed a silly time for a funeral but he dared say the folk concerned had their reasons.

The rest of his load would provide the decorations at a reception the next morning for some visitors from Cloughton's twin town, Pont d'Agneau. There'd be another team of gossipy ladies this evening, busy in the Town Hall. Chrysanthemums for them and one of the big boxes of greenery.

The mobile phone in his pocket rang and he heard his employer's irate tones. 'Where the hell are you? I've had two calls from Doreen saying you aren't there yet!'

The driver thought quickly. 'I've been held up by an accident in the High Street. They closed it off.' He'd be too idle to check!

'Well, get a move on now. Oh, and Carl's free to service the vans tonight. Park yours on the forecourt when you get back and you'll have to get the bus home.'

'I've to do the Town Hall first.'

'Hellfire, man! Where have you been all afternoon? Just get your bloody foot down now . . .'

The driver stopped listening to his boss's invective. He glanced at his watch and panicked. Why did it have to be tonight that Carl wanted the van? Usually he took it straight home, listened yet again to his neighbour's unfunny references to the garden ornament on his drive and devoured the huge tea his mum had got ready for him. Now she'd have left for her dressmaking class when he got back and his food would be drying up in the oven. He'd have to try to get her a microwave, although it was safer to go for smaller things. You wouldn't be able to get a microwave into even a greenery box.

And where was he going to hide today's box of 'pickings' overnight? He could hardly carry it home on the bus. His employer's angry tirade seemed to be over now and he slipped the silent phone back into his pocket. Perhaps the old devil was so bad-tempered because his name was always being ridiculed. The driver could certainly sympathize with him there.

8

In the end, he decided to push the box under a table at the back of the little room where Doreen made up the wreaths. If Mr Flowers – or the police – found out what he had been doing this afternoon, she would be making up one for him!

Chapter One

A good many friends and relatives of the late Edgar James Smith had chosen, on this Tuesday afternoon, to pay their last respects to him by attending his funeral service at St Barnabas'. As the clock on the tower chimed the quarter they turned the page of their Books of Common Prayer and saw with relief that their sheepish progress through the unfamiliar ceremony in this alien building was almost at an end.

There would be the follow-up at the crematorium, of course, before they could relax at the knees-up at his daughter Diane's house, but that would be more official, less churchy. They'd be able to cope with that. They cheered up as a splendidly coped and vestmented vicar intoned his penultimate phrase. 'Man that is born of woman hath but a short time to live.'

Edgar, though, had had a reasonable innings. A fatal heart attack at sixty-nine was better than ten extra years' suffering from something slow and painful. One member of that reluctant congregation had indeed 'but a short time' remaining. No more than a few hours, in fact. At the moment, though, with no premonition of an untimely end, that person was rendering the final hymn with an almost unseemly gusto.

'Swift to its close ebbs out life's little day;
Earth's joys grow dim, its glories pass away;
Change and decay in all around I see . . .'

Lorraine was not impressed with the sentiments of the

10

funeral hymns but, if sing them she must, then she would do it with a will. She knew that she was embarrassing Philip, towering on one side of her, and amusing Donna on the other.

Her father had not changed or decayed when she had taken her last look at him. He had seemed to be peacefully asleep, and seeing him at rest in his coffin had helped to erase the picture of him in the agonizing throes of the seizure that had killed him. What, she wondered, did being dead mean? Where was Dad now? And did having such questions in her head mean that she believed in an afterlife? Maybe she did. Certainly, it was more feasible that her cheerful, energetic father was making an impact elsewhere than that he'd just ceased to exist.

She glanced across at her sister who was surreptitiously checking her make-up with the help of a small mirror. Yes, Diane's lipstick had bled into the crevices in her top lip. Lorraine smiled spitefully and returned to her self-examination. So, there was a serious side to her mind after all. Diane called her shallow and frivolous, yet here she was meditating on heaven and hell whilst her sister was merely titivating.

Lorraine was glad that they had settled on St Barnabas' for the service. The church that Diane went to at Easter and Christmas, and referred to as hers, had been 'refurbished' and was now more like a second-rate hotel foyer than a place of worship. This was a 'proper' church with uncomfortable dark wooden pews and a bare, stone-flagged floor except for narrow tracks of blue carpet across the back, down the aisle and wherever else the worshippers had to walk. The Mothers' Union banner, propped in the front corner beside the Communion table, brightened the scene with a splash of scarlet and gold.

When they had come to see the vicar to arrange things there had been white posies on the window sills. These had disappeared and today the church was decorated with magnificent red and white pedestal displays provided by the florist Diane had employed. Lorraine thought Dad would have preferred the posies.

11

As the hymn finished, Lorraine made to sit down but a poke from Philip brought her to her feet again. The pall-bearers were hoisting the coffin to their shoulders once more. When the coffin had reached the door they would be able to start moving.

She glanced impatiently at her sister and brother-in-law who were now kneeling at the open end of the pew in a semblance of prayer and blocking the way out. Diane and Barry were no more in the habit of praying than she was herself. Still, at least she could turn and look round now without being frowned on.

She was glad to see old Walter Denby, Dad's chess partner and his senior by some fifteen years. He had come dressed in his accustomed manner since he always wore a dark suit and a tie. Two ancient aunts also looked much as they normally did as their wardrobes consisted entirely of floor-length black skirts and long-sleeved black blouses. The rest of the congregation looked unlike themselves in a motley array of garments, varying in subdued hue from deepest black, through shades of grey to violet and occasional lilac. Some were so ill-fitting as to have obviously been borrowed for the occasion.

Diane had realized that the toes of her precious new shoes were resting unprotected on the stone floor, beyond the range of the strip of carpet that ran the length of the pew beneath their feet. Hastily assuming a sitting position again she rubbed at them to the detriment of a lace-edged handkerchief. Since the pretty embroidered scrap had not been required to dry tears, Lorraine was glad to see it had found a purpose.

As they followed their father's remains to the porch, the two sisters found their hands being clasped, first by a rather unctuous vicar and then by the crowd of mourners that surged from behind and surrounded them. Both attempted to look simultaneously sad and brave and both felt extremely ill at ease.

When she could manage it, Lorraine liked to be fair. She knew that Diane, for all her affectation and in spite of her having used their father's obsequies as a showcase for her wealth, would grieve, even weep, for him in private. She would do the same herself.

Perched on his organ stool, behind the second row of decani choir stalls, Cavill Jackson came to the end of the short voluntary that Diane Bates had chosen for the end of the service. He'd guided her to the music of Henry Purcell and tried to persuade her, if she was really set on a choral item, to choose a very short one. The setting to the one sentence, 'Hear my prayer, O Lord, and let my crying come unto thee', had been his recommendation.

Diane, however, had wanted more notes for her money and had insisted on another. Cavill wondered what his choirboys had made of:

> Man that is born of woman
> Hath but a short time to live
> And is full of misery.
> He cometh up
> And is cut down like a flower.
> He fleeth as it were a shadow
> And ne'er continueth in one stay.

What had the congregation made of it, come to that?

In mischievous mood, and to tease Mrs Bates, he had suggested that the head chorister should supply a solemn drumbeat, as in the original score to the processional music. She had been ecstatic and immediately insisted on it. He'd noticed today that this had reduced Lorraine, the deceased's other daughter, to hysterical giggles and hoped her friends and relatives would attribute her tears to a more appropriate cause.

By now, the church having been full, only about a third of the congregation had made their way to the porch. Rather than improvise on the short work he had just finished, he decided to hurry the rest along with his favourite Lefebure-Wely piece, a lively sortie that Lorraine had wanted for the service and that Diane Bates had rejected as disrespectful.

13

He began to play at top speed – oompah, oompah – then the ridiculous tune began on top to be played with an ultra-light touch. Now the series of slow notes, the last one to be held longer until he let it slide into a new tempo and allowed the melody to swing to and fro between the rafters. He was afraid for a moment that the cracking pace he had set himself might cause him to fudge some of the demi-semi-quavers. His hands were well practised and safe, though, and all was well.

Pity he had to go to the funeral bash at Diane's house later on and have his hand smacked for it. Never mind. The fun had been worth it.

As the family party moved out behind the coffin, Donna slipped out of the front pew, where she had been sitting with her mother. She squeezed into the space next to the aisle on a pew several rows back. Her father made room for her and she watched contentedly from there. She saw with satisfaction that Auntie Diane was annoyed with her for moving. Her mother merely checked with a glance that her father was now in charge.

She blinked as the slow and solemn music came to an end and the organ began on something lively and loud. The man had the right idea. Grandad would have loved this one. She stuck her head out into the aisle until she was able to look at the organist and was surprised. He didn't look tall and was only thin – too weedy to make such a crashing noise on that great elephant of an instrument.

She turned her attention to the church building and became mesmerized by it. Why candles when there were those great fancy lights? She liked them, though – the smell as well as the flame. She liked the coloured windows too, even though it made things a bit dark. She drew her feet back out of the aisle as one of the fleeing congregation stumbled over them. Where had all these people come from? Grandad would have laughed at the clothes they were wearing and the way they were trying to look sad.

14

Her father bent to whisper. 'They'll be waiting for you to get in the first car.'

'You should be in that one as well.'

He smiled and shook his head. Donna was impatient with her father for submitting to her aunt's treatment of him but felt a bit sorry for her too. She could see how everyone liked her mother better than Diane. It made her aunt want a big house and fancy clothes and whatever else made her seem important in the family. All Auntie Diane's posh friends were shocked that Donna's mum and dad were not married. This meant that Diane couldn't invite her father to the house much. But then she was scared of being called a snob so she couldn't ignore him either. Why did grown-ups make things so complicated? Poor old things.

She grinned at her father mischievously. 'Can I come in the Yellow Peril with you instead of the funeral car?'

He shrugged. 'If you can take the aggro it'll cause, I suppose I can.'

Lorraine stepped forward, with Diane, out of the shelter of the porch, through the fine but drenching rain, to climb into the first of the silver limousines that purred now to the foot of the stone steps. The funeral director and his assistant held huge black umbrellas over the daughters and son-in-law of the deceased. Under their shelter, Diane paused to check that Nick was not hovering in an attempt to intrude into this intimate group.

To annoy Diane and Barry, Lorraine would have invited him to join them, but she knew his pride would have prevented his accepting. In any case, she could see him now, twenty yards away, climbing into his ancient Renault, half canary yellow, half covered in rust. She imagined he would take a perverse pleasure in being the inappropriate final vehicle in this convoy of gleaming grey. She knew too that he would prefer to be alone with his genuine sorrow for Edgar's passing.

*   *   *

Nick had certainly shed real tears for Edgar during the service. Now, however, his mind was preoccupied with his car. He prayed he could start it up without too much attention being attracted by its rattles and bangs. As he nursed it along the route to Elm Road, he reflected on the irony of his situation. He didn't want to arrive there and one of the reasons he had come was because he knew his host and hostess didn't want him. There were other reasons, though. His respect for Edgar Smith had been whole-hearted. The old man had deserved the tribute of a full church. Then, of course, he had to keep an eye on Lorraine and he never turned down the chance of time with Donna.

He felt sorry for Diane. Every occasion was her show-case, her chance to shine, but she never succeeded in making the impression she wanted, maybe needed. She had furnished her house at great expense but with considerable lack of judgement. The effect of her designer clothes was spoiled by her stocky figure, further padded by indulgent dining in all the right restaurants.

He supposed Lorraine was no longer the sylph she had been when he lived with her and Donna was conceived. She was still effortlessly attractive, though, because of her zest and enthusiasm for everything, her quick mind and her appetite for all experiences. Above all, for her complete disregard of other people's judgements of her. Nick wondered, yet again, what had gone wrong between Lorraine and himself. He had realized that they were increasingly involved in petty squabbles, but he had been hurt and shocked when she had suggested a separation. He still didn't quite understand it. Lorraine was not a quitter but he supposed she had been worn down by Philip's tantrums, her pregnancy and looking after Donna who had been a fractious baby. Maybe she had suffered from post-natal depression, though Lorraine herself would have scorned both the name and the concept.

Today he'd been glad to see that she wasn't dressed as bizarrely as he had feared. There was neither funereal black nor areas of distracting bare flesh. Of course she

16

would pay proper respect to her father. He should have trusted her. They would laugh together later about the display of insincere grief represented by black armbands, even a black hat with a veil.

Nick shook himself. If he were to fulfil everyone's expectations of him this evening, he had better get a move on and offer some practical help. He parked the Renault with a word of praise to the patron saint of geriatric vehicles and went indoors.

Cavill arrived a little late at the reception in Elm Road, so that he could hide in the crowd and avoid Diane's complaints. He discovered, to his amusement, that there was nothing to worry about. When she had heard several approving comments on his mischievous choice of sortie, she had evidently decided to claim credit for its being the finale to the service. 'I thought it would be a good idea to finish with something modern,' he heard her explaining to a blue-rinsed lady as he passed them.

His hostess had also made much of his own reputation, stressing his connection with her father and its reflected glory on herself. Two people asked him how long he and Diane had been friends, obviously wondering why he had not been paraded before them till now. Those she had impressed came to congratulate him on the service music, contriving to mention the musicians in their own families and their own musical prowess in their younger days.

A more discerning guest came up to congratulate him on his boys' choir. Cavill accepted his compliments graciously, describing his own pleasure in teaching them. 'The lads don't realize what powerful instruments they have when they first arrive.'

'Instruments?'

'Their voices. They have to learn to use them just as much as they need to learn the rudiments of violin or clarinet playing.'

'Hadn't thought of that. My young grandson's one of them – James Denning.'

17

Cavill beamed. 'He's one of my best.'

His companion looked proud but doubtful. 'They have to give up a hell of a lot of time getting to your standard. I worry about the lad's general development, as a person. He doesn't have much time for messing about with his pals, kicking a football around.'

'James's pals are in the choir. And what else would he have been doing that would give him as much satisfaction? Besides, are you telling me they're not enjoying themselves?'

Defeated by Cavill's beaming enthusiasm, the man decided it was time he 'mingled' and disappeared into the crowd round the drinks table. His place at Cavill's side was taken by a vigorous-looking elderly lady. 'Don't you find,' she demanded, after introducing herself and thanking him, 'that all the technicalities you have to bear in mind as you play spoil the magic of the music for you?'

Cavill shook his head. 'No. They're ingredients of the spell. When it works, you don't remember all the dismembered frogs and newts and toads in the recipe.' The old lady looked puzzled, but a small crowd had now gathered around Cavill and the questions, revealing various degrees of intelligence and musicality, were coming thick and fast.

'How much leeway do you have with music?'

'None.'

Then a welcome honest comment: 'Can't say I followed much of what was going on but we appreciate someone of your eminence taking trouble . . .' Honest, but also embarrassing. Whatever had Diane been inventing?

He was thankful that the next speaker was old Walter Denby who played the euphonium in Cloughton's senior citizens' orchestra. The two of them discussed its doings happily until a prosperous-looking individual, vainly trying to disguise his flat local vowels, asked Cavill, 'Do you have an input into any other musical charities?'

'Charities!' This roar from Walter told Cavill the defence of the orchestra was in safe hands. With a wink at the old man, he escaped to find food and drink. He noticed with

18

some pleasure that the bright-eyed child he had noticed in church, who had hung on the edge of the group he had left, had now followed him. In spite of her inappropriate, trendy clothing and beringed ears, she had a sharp, intelligent face, and seemed on the point of addressing him. He reached for a glass of squash and handed it to her.

She smiled her thanks. 'I should be serving you. I promised to be a waitress, but I wanted to ask you some things.' He waited. 'Who wrote the jazzy music?' She didn't need to elaborate.

'It certainly wasn't jazz, but I know what you mean. It was a Frenchman in the nineteenth century, a child prodigy as an organist. I believe he gave his first recital at the age of eight. His father ended up as organist at a famous church called St Sulpice.'

'That's in Paris, isn't it?'

'You know it?'

She shook her head. 'I haven't been there but it's where all the stuff in *The Da Vinci Code* happened and I've read that. There was a picture. It's very big and important-looking but it doesn't look like an English church.'

'I suppose not. It was considered very fashionable. The Marquis de Sade was baptised there and it's where Victor Hugo got married.'

'Who to?'

Cavill laughed. 'You've got me there. Its choir was very famous and its organ is the largest in Europe.'

Donna looked impressed. 'Have you played it?'

Cavill closed his eyes for a second, in reverent memory. 'Just once. I knew you were enjoying the E flat sortie. I could see you through my mirror.'

'What do you have a mirror for? To spy on us?'

'No, but that's what I do. It's meant to show me any signals the vicar wants to give me and the head choirboy can use it to see any signal I want to give him.'

'Right. Do you always play the music you like or does it sometimes have to be stuff you hate?'

He winked at her. 'A bit of both. When I'm as famous as

19

your aunt seems to think I am, then I'll be able to do just as I like.'

Unable to reach the table over the heads of taller guests, she handed him her empty glass. 'If I was an organist, playing that piece we had today would be my favourite musical joke. It says, "Come on, hurry up and get outside."'

Cavill grinned delightedly. 'You're absolutely right. That's exactly what the composer meant it to say. It's a sortie.'

'Yes, you said. That's French for leaving, going out. That's what I'd like to do, but I'd better collect some more empty glasses like I promised Auntie Diane.'

Cavill thought he had better 'mingle' as that same lady had commanded him.

Glenda Grant stood by the doorway into the Bateses' main reception room and wondered how soon she could decently get away. Other people would invent a further fictitious engagement and be able to disappear gracefully, even collecting grateful thanks from their hosts for appearing at their function at all.

She was resentful because she was yet again representing her immediate family at an event that none of them wanted to attend. Toni and Victor easily managed to avoid such affairs. Their facile excuses – sometimes half-truths, often complete fabrications – never troubled them. Something inside Glenda, maybe genes from her Wee Free grandmother, obliged her to speak the truth.

Across the room, she could see the poor organist chap being mobbed by the more foolish of Diane's friends. At least she had a fellow sufferer – and there was a gleam of amusement to be gained from seeing someone like Diane getting excited about organ music. Of course, the music was not what was causing the excitement, though Glenda had heard the man play and admired him. The organ was not her favourite instrument but Cavill Jackson was a local celebrity and he had introduced her to some sounds she had not realized it could make. All that made him important to Diane was that his doings were reported frequently in the local rag and, from time to time, in the broadsheets.

There was a modicum of entertainment too in the antics of Diane's sister. Glenda's disapproval of Lorraine was well mixed with both envy and an odd kind of respect. Lorraine would never put up with Toni's tantrums or Victor's humiliating liaisons. The humiliation seemed to be only hers. Victor seemed quite pleased with his reputation as 'a bit of a lad'. What cliché, she wondered, did people use to describe her?

She closed her eyes, realizing that she did have a slight headache. Perhaps even someone as unfortunately honest as herself could exaggerate her discomfort slightly. But she knew she wouldn't leave until her hostess indicated that the proceedings were at an end.

Barry Bates sank wearily into the soft folds of the leather sofa in the hall. It was Diane's latest acquisition and there wasn't enough room for it. He had known, as soon as she saw its twin in the vast hall of the Grants' house on the occasion of Toni's engagement party, that Diane would have to have one. There, it looked magnificent. Here, squashed between their hall stand and the chest of drawers that doubled as a telephone table, it made their hall, spacious though it was, look poky. In front of the radiator had been the only possible place to fit it in and the beautiful leather was drying out as well as absorbing the heat that should have circulated through the house.

Resignedly, he watched Nick Felling and his nephew, Philip, help Diane's sister up the stairs. It had been a matter of when, not if, Lorraine got drunk. In Barry's opinion, Diane was making just as much of a fool of herself. This was not the occasion for anything but a quiet and abstemious drink and some talk about Edgar.

Barry willed the hours and minutes away till they all went home. Small parties of close friends were fine, but he hated having his house full of people he hadn't the time to talk to as individuals. He wouldn't resent it so much if he thought that Diane was enjoying them or that any of them cared about her. These affairs were just an endless charade of friendship in which she displayed her possessions rather than herself.

Would she have been happier, had real friends, had a chance to be who she really was if she'd married a poor man? Not that Diane had ever been poor – at least, not since she was very small, before Edgar had become so successful. He supposed she wouldn't remember those days as well as Lorraine did. Certainly, she never spoke of them.

It seemed odd that the two of them had been produced and raised by the same two parents. Sisters were expected to be close to each other, but there was no real reason why they should be. Siblings were often very different. They shared some experiences and conditions of their child-hood, but their genetic differences and their position in the family meant they saw the same situations in very differ-ent ways. Parents didn't give them the same treatment, except superficially. It was in ways that weren't always apparent to casual observers that differences were made. The children themselves were very aware of them.

How extraordinary it was of Edgar to be so cruel to Diane now – if, of course, you could trust old Walter Denby, in his cups, to know what he was talking about. Barry was horribly afraid it was true, though. People became indiscreet when they were drunk, rather than dis-honest. They invented their falsehoods when they had all their wits about them.

Perhaps Diane's mother had drummed her own false values into her daughter. Lorraine had been so much Edgar's favourite that May and her younger daughter had been thrown together and Diane still missed May more than she would now miss her father. Would she miss her possessions more than either of them – and would she consider that her husband had let her down just as her father was doing even now?

22

All he could manage for her now was the best salvage operation he was capable of. Barry shook his head to clear it. Perhaps he'd drunk rather too much himself. He'd sort out his problems in the morning.

Her last hours almost up, Lorraine lay on the bed in her sister's spare room, giggling to herself. In disgrace again! Was she supposed to lie here and repent?

She fingered the lace cover that Nick had draped over her. Diane would have a fit if she knew he'd used it. She'd have considered a couple of old towels more suitable, or a dust sheet out of the loft. This room was just typical of Diane. Peach and cream were Diane colours. Even the pictures on the wall had been chosen to fit the scheme. Her sister was probably not actually aware of what was in them. They were just part of her interior designer's 'tasteful' luxury.

It looked as though Diane had moved the one that used to be over the mantelpiece. She had her rooms decorated so frequently that the space it had left was only a very slightly different colour from the rest of the wall. She knew the picture had been there though. It had been one of the few in the house that she liked.

She'd have a look at the rest in a little while, but not until the room had stopped spinning quite so fast, nor until her legs would hold her upright. It had been a good party. The music the little red-haired organist had played them out with had put everyone in the right mood for it. That's how she'd like to go herself, when her time came, all flags flying, the way she lived. Perhaps she'd put something in her will about it. She believed you could do that.

She'd seen Diane's lips tighten as they stood together in the porch. As the preposterous notes had filled the cavernous space above them, her own heart had lifted. She'd wanted to dance up the aisle in response. Her lips had twitched as she'd seen her sister's face, pinched white with fury. Now, she felt sorry for her. There wasn't much joy for Diane because she hadn't got any joy in her.

She had to allow that Diane was a good caterer. Between them they had given Dad a good send-off. Diane had provided the setting and she herself had provided the atmosphere, livened things up a bit. Dad would have been grateful to both of them.

When Lorraine heard the door handle being tried, she was surprised. Nick usually gave her longer to sober up. She turned her head quickly, then wished she had been more careful. When the mad rushing behind her eyes had subsided sufficiently for her to open them again, she grinned shamefacedly at her visitor.

Lorraine felt only slightly puzzled when the pillow was picked up and only mildly alarmed as it came towards her face. Was this a joke?

She had her answer in just a second or two as the blackness behind her eyes turned to redness. She tried to take deep breaths but her lungs received only dust and fragments of feathers. She fought as long as her strength lasted but soon she could feel the tissues of her mouth and throat swelling, narrowing the blocked airways. Finally came blessed oblivion.

After several more seconds the pillow was replaced to the side of its victim's head, only a centimetre or two from its original position. The door closed quietly but even a loud slam would not have disturbed Lorraine now.

Chapter Two

Back home, his hard day completed, tankard at his elbow, Detective Chief Inspector Benedict Mitchell prepared to enjoy his two rewards – sampling the first of his latest batch of homebrew and watching the eighty minutes of the first rugby match of the season. His ten-year-old son had relieved his mother of the duty of making the recording, so Mitchell was assured that the machine would not have been tuned inadvertently to the wrong channel. He was sorry, though, that Declan was not, so far, excited by the egg-shaped ball. Caitlin, two and a half years younger, would sometimes watch for a short time, asking questions that showed an understanding of the rudiments of the game.

Mitchell's wife had left the living room clean and tidy before escaping from the match and taking a book to their bedroom. He had spent twenty minutes improving on this and achieving the pristine order in which he felt comfortable before indulging himself. The house had settled itself for the evening. Just one lamp was lit to challenge the fading light and none of his four children was disturbing the peace. Even Sinead, the night-bird twin, had run out of excuses to call downstairs.

Mitchell was convinced that his younger daughter would become an actress. He and Ginny had determined so often that the next trip downstairs after she had been settled in bed would land her in big trouble. Then the request or problem she produced was so plausibly explained, soulful eyes and dramatic gestures filling in where the vocabulary of a five-year-old proved inadequate, that it won her the five more minutes' attention she wanted. None of this nonsense ever disturbed Michael. He had probably become used, in the womb, to sleeping through her histrionics and now continued to do so in their shared bedroom.

Mitchell hoped none of his family would be disturbed by Jonathan Davies's high-pitched, manic commentary on the match. As a precaution, he turned the volume down before slipping the tape into the machine. Then he kicked off his slippers, lifted his feet on to the sofa and savoured the first swallow from his tankard.

The telephone rang.

'It's Sergeant Powers, sir.'

'It's my precious evening off, Magic. This had better be at least a murder.'

'Well, we've got a body, sir.'

'I'm waiting for the "but". Has Dr Holland seen it?'

'I – er – think he's on his way, sir.'

Mitchell sighed. That meant no one had summoned him yet. 'Give him a call on his mobile, Magic, and suggest he gets a move on.'

He jotted down the details he was given, collected his coat and keys, and was glad to find that the day's rain had relented to a fine drizzle. Driving through the centre of the town, which was quiet for the moment, he reached Meadowbank, the sought-after area that encompassed Elm Road.

Turning into the drive of number 8 he saw that several cars were already parked in front of the house. Most of them were fairly new and expensive-looking but he squeezed his Cavalier into a space between an ancient Renault 4 and the wall. He paused to examine the house. Darkness was falling fast but the imposing size could still be appreciated. Light spilled across a terrace as the officer who had noted his arrival opened the front door and came to meet him.

He was not surprised to recognize DC Shakila Nazir. She had as good a nose for a meaty case as he'd always had himself and contrived, by means he'd never fathomed, always to be on the scene at the beginning of it. He grinned at her. 'Can you put me in the picture? All I know is that the call came from the householder, a Mr Bates, and that the deceased is his sister-in-law. Who else is here?'

'On the team, you mean?' Shakila named her three colleagues who were presently in charge in the house. 'There's only the four of us, apart from the funeral party.'

Mitchell blinked. 'They were here for a funeral?' She nodded. 'So where are they now?'

'We've collected them all into the two big reception rooms.'

They both turned as they heard a car door slam behind them and Dr Holland joined them. Mitchell offered the desk sergeant a silent apology before greeting the pathologist. The rain had now almost given up but the clean smell of wet earth filled the air as they conferred briefly. Mitchell learned from him that one of the funeral guests was a hospital consultant and that it had been on his advice that the police had been called. A stroke of luck – provided the two medics could tolerate each other.

Mitchell paused in the hall, brushing from his coat beads of moisture that had formed a furry wetness before the fabric absorbed them. He looked around him, taking in the gracious proportions. It was not an ancient building but late Victorian money had probably built it when the textile industry flourished in Cloughton. The furniture was not appropriate. The pieces were expensive and aggressively modern, the light waxed wood of the hall stand and the huge chest of drawers being made to feel unwelcome by the magnificent mahogany staircase rails. The scents of savoury food and good wines and spirits mingled with those of flowers and perfumed cosmetics.

Shakila volunteered that the body had not been discovered until the party was breaking up. 'A few people had left but not many. I get the impression that the parties here are good with expensive drink and food.'

The pathologist was anxious to get his job started without having to attend a mini-briefing. 'Shall we have a quick look for ourselves and then talk to this medic?'

Mitchell wondered how he could look, quickly or otherwise, through his thick, bottle-bottomed lenses and see what he was carving up. Maybe they should be thankful that he had chosen to operate on dead bodies. In spite of his suspect sight and his unfortunate brand of humour, Holland had an intelligent face and already enjoyed the good opinion of officers in their area whom the Cloughton force respected.

Mitchell nodded and they crossed to the stairs, avoiding a sleek black cat, sprawled on the carpet as though it had been spilt there. He let Shakila escort them to the room where the dead woman lay. As usual, she made herself one of the party and followed them in without waiting for permission. The three of them stood for some moments, looking down at the bed. A strong stench of vomit filled the room, almost eclipsing the reek of alcohol.

'She's not exactly conventionally dressed for a funeral,' the pathologist remarked mildly. 'She's probably a dyed blonde.'

Mitchell parted the short, sleeked-back hair to examine the roots. 'I don't think so.'

'She doesn't look very old,' Shakila ventured. When neither of her companions replied, she half-withdrew her remark. 'With her face all blotched like that, you can't really tell, though.'

'Look at her hands,' Dr Holland suggested. All three of them looked. The hands were large with square-tipped fingers, and two prominent veins across the back of each.

'We won't have to guess,' Mitchell observed. 'Most of the people downstairs will be happy to tell us.'

Dr Holland turned happily back to his lifeless patient. 'Hm. Warm, and just a little stiffness in the jaw.' He looked up. 'The early Greeks and Egyptians, you know, believed rigor could make a corpse sit up in bed.'

Mitchell's heart sank. This was his first experience of the new pathologist in action. He had heard that this successor to Dr Ledgard, now retired, saw entertaining the force as one of his duties – or did he think he was educating them?

Mitchell's glare evidently told Holland that Shakila

would be a more appreciative audience. He grinned at her. 'In twelve hours, you know, you can rest the head of a corpse on one chair and his feet on another and his body stays flat like a bewitched volunteer in a magician's show.' He waited for some appreciation of this observation, but Shakila too had noted Mitchell's glare and kept her eyes fixed on Lorraine Conroy's still form. Defeated, the pathologist gave a running commentary on the accumulation of carbon dioxide and lack of oxygen that had led to the swelling of veins and tissues and the production of petechiae. 'Those are –'

'I know, the little dark bruises.'

Dr Holland frowned at Shakila. 'They aren't bruises but they are those dark marks on her face and scalp. The pressure of the pillow stopped the blood in the veins from returning to the heart. They filled to bursting point, then the blood escaped into the surrounding tissues.'

To avoid the rest of the lecture, Shakila asked hurriedly, 'Why are her nose and mouth and forehead white?'

'Think about it.' The pathologist helped the DC's thinking along by pinching her arm hard between his own finger and thumb.

Shakila stepped back, looking indignant until she saw the point of the attack. 'You mean someone pressed something hard over her face and stopped . . .?'

Mitchell asked, 'How long would it take?'

'Probably two or three minutes for her to become unconscious and four to five minutes for her to die.'

'Someone took an awful risk then.'

Holland nodded. 'She could have died much more quickly, of vagal inhibition.'

'Frightened to death, you mean?'

'Yes, but she wasn't. There are all the superficial physical signs of death from asphyxia. She could have hastened her death by struggling, though. That uses up the oxygen in the blood, but the killer couldn't have counted on that happening.'

'So we are looking for a killer?'

'You can't quote me until I've done the PM, but, for practical purposes, yes, you are.'

Dr Holland returned to his prying into and prodding of the corpse so, followed by Shakila, Mitchell left him to it and went downstairs. In the hall he found a uniformed man now guarding the front door. He reported briefly. 'Only officials in or out, sir, since I arrived.'

'How many guests would you say?'

'Forty-four of them.' He indicated the reception room doors with a jerk of his head. 'The two officers have been taking names and addresses.'

'Right, thanks.' Mitchell turned to Shakila and indicated the rooms in which the guests were herded. 'Who've we got in there?'

'A uniform I don't know and Caroline. By the way, Cavill is one of the guests. Lucky for us.'

Mitchell repressed his whoop of delight and said only, 'But not for him. I'd better start by talking to Dr Scott.'

'Mr Scott, sir. He's a surgeon.'

'Thank you.' The rueful tone had told Mitchell that Shakila had made the same blunder and been put in her place.

Since it was empty, he decided to make the kitchen his temporary office. Mr Scott obeyed his summons promptly and the two surveyed each other over a table piled high with empty bottles and glasses. Mitchell saw a bustling, rather pompous man, a little shorter than the average with thinning and greying hair.

After a few minutes he liked Scott better as he realized his huffing and puffing was less to emphasize his own importance and more because he was asthmatic. He let his witness repeat the information he had already heard about the white pressure marks on the victim's face.

'It could have happened accidentally if she'd been lying face down but she was on her back.'

'So, what did you do?'

Scott shrugged. 'Made sure there was nothing I could do to help her, of course. Then I went down and told them.'

'Told them what?'

'That she was dead.'

'Not that she was murdered?'

He shook his head. 'I wasn't a hundred per cent sure of that. I won't be personally till your pathologist has analysed the inhaled matter in the lungs.'

'All right.' Mitchell moved some bottles so that he could see the whole of the doctor's face. 'How did the other guests react?'

'There was a stunned silence. I suppose they all assumed that she'd died because of what she'd drunk.'

'Then what?'

'Mr Conroy and Mr Felling came towards me to go upstairs. I wouldn't let them. I asked Mr Bates, whose house we're in, to call the police.'

Mitchell glanced round to assure himself that the uniformed officer's shorthand was keeping up with Neville Scott's revelations. Satisfied, he continued. 'Who are Mr Felling and Mr Conroy?'

The doctor smiled mirthlessly. 'You'd better concentrate hard. It's complicated. Philip Conroy is Lorraine's son, her illegitimate son, born when she was seventeen and still at school. This farce of a party followed Edgar Smith's funeral. Lorraine was Edgar Smith's daughter. His other daughter, the younger, is Diane Bates, our hostess.' Scott paused to make use of his inhaler before continuing. The uniformed officer gratefully augmented his notes.

'Lorraine was married for a while, very happily, I believe, but her husband died. Later, she and Mr Felling – er . . . got together.'

Mitchell paused to assimilate this, checking his information aloud. 'Edgar Smith died – natural causes, we hope. Daughter two, Diane Bates, gives him a good send-off. Daughter one, with interesting love life and illegitimate offspring, gets herself murdered at aforementioned send-off. Thanks. Go on.'

31

But Scott abandoned his account to ask a question. 'Are you going to interview the girl, Donna?'

'Donna?'

'Daughter of Lorraine and Nicholas Felling.'

'After they'd – er, got together?' When Scott disdained to answer, Mitchell asked, 'How old is she?'

'Twelve or thirteen.'

'Then, properly chaperoned, we shall certainly expect her to tell us all she can. Are you opposed to our questioning her – as her doctor?'

He shook his head. 'Not at all. She'll thoroughly enjoy it. You just need to be warned not to take anything she says too seriously. She's apt to – well, fantasize a bit. Reads a lot, lives inside her head and says disconcerting things.'

'Disconcerting?'

'Well, I suppose they're often uncomfortably accurate.'

Mitchell nodded. 'Thank you. It sounds as though she's just the sort of person we want to talk to, but we'll bear your warning in mind.' It struck him that Scott's observations on the family situation were somewhat detached and he asked, 'Are you here as a family friend?'

He smiled. 'No, I'm here because Edgar Smith was my patient in the Infirmary between his first heart attack and his death. We were doing tests to assess the feasibility of bypass surgery but then he had a second, fatal attack. I'm here, like the vicar and the organist, because this is a middle-class family that accepts its social responsibilities.'

'So how do you know so much of the family history?'

For the first time, Scott looked slightly ill at ease. 'I know – or knew – Lorraine herself rather better. We have a common interest in amateur drama. She enjoyed actually treading the boards. I'm just a sort of patron. Lorraine was a good actress. She was forty but she played a girl of twenty in our last production and was utterly convincing. It was called *Not Quite a Lady*. Lorraine said that was a perfect description of herself.'

Mitchell asked, with real curiosity, 'You mean you supported them financially? What made you sufficiently interested to do that?'

Scott became pompous again. 'Two things. First, I'll support any venture in which young people work together towards a positive end. Then, I have a personal interest. My son is their producer and it's his ambition eventually to direct his own company professionally.'

He glanced at his watch, then, seeing Mitchell had noticed, apologized. 'I realize I have to tell you all I know, but I'm due in theatre in just over seven hours.'

Mitchell had no wish to be responsible, even indirectly, for more deaths. 'All right. Just two more quick questions and I'll save the rest. How did Lorraine's son and Mr Felling react to your refusing to let them see the body?'

'Mr Felling was upset – but by the news, not by being kept downstairs. He couldn't speak, was trying not to weep. Philip was calm. I think he had faced the idea already that his mother's drinking could kill her. He asked if she'd choked on her own vomit.'

'So, he'd seen the body already?'

'No, but Diane had. She went up to the spare room to get some trays. She thought Lorraine was just asleep and came down in a rare old temper because her sister had thrown up over the bedding. I went up with my doctor's hat on, but there was nothing I could do. What's the other question?'

'An open-ended one. Is there anything you've noticed that you think I ought to know about?'

Scott considered for a few moments and then smiled. 'Yes, I think you ought to know that you look completely exhausted, and that it is my professional opinion that a few hours' sleep will help you with your investigation more than anything any of us might tell you tonight.'

Mitchell had thanked Mr Scott both for his information and for his advice. Nevertheless, before dismissing everyone except the constables who were to watch the premises until first light, he went back upstairs. He broke the seal that Dr Holland had put on the spare bedroom door and went in to spend a few minutes alone with Lorraine's

33

body. Now his victim had a name she could also reveal her personality. A great many facts would be discovered about her in the following days but all of them would be filtered through the opinions, preferences and prejudices of the people who offered them.

Mitchell felt himself warming to the woman who had stood by the baby she had conceived as a schoolgirl and survived the ending of a happy marriage caused by the premature death of the man she loved.

He examined the woman's clothing, so despised by Ray Holland. The colours were acceptable in every sense, dove grey and deep purple. They were much more suited to delicate colouring than black. That was considered a bit over the top these days anyway. The skirt was short but the legs were good; the neckline plunged but the bosom was worthy. The face had been attractive and had probably been quite skilfully made up. The application of fine cotton and feathers had removed some of the make-up and smudged some more.

Mitchell's's keen sense of smell, having accustomed itself to the vomit and the now fainter hint of spirits, had picked up a third scent. It was Lorraine's perfume, flowery but cheap and chemical, hardly in keeping with the general picture he was building up.

There was a tap on the door and it opened to reveal the scene of crime team. He nodded a temporary farewell to his latest victim and went downstairs where Shakila hovered in the hall waiting for orders. Mitchell dismissed her.

'You'll need your rest tonight.' He began to enumerate her tasks for the next morning.

She grinned at him. 'There isn't a murder till the pathologist says so.'

There was no answering smile. 'Yes, and by lunchtime we'll not be able to do anything unless the super says so. Let's be having you.'

Mitchell opened the door of the large reception room to the

right of the front door with some compunction. It was late and these people were tired. They had all of them suffered a double bereavement and some of them at least were genuinely grieving. He caught his intended victim's eye and Cavill Jackson came out looking resigned.

'This is becoming a habit, you know.'

Diane Bates, following Cavill into the hall, approached Mitchell with an icy glare. 'These people are my guests. Mr Jackson is a churchman and an organist of some renown. I can't have him hauled out of my drawing room like this without even a polite request – as if he's a criminal.'

Cavill, glancing from her to Mitchell and back again, remarked, 'Don't worry. I'm used to it.'

Bemused, Diane turned back to Mitchell. 'I know you have a job to do . . .'

Cavill managed a half-smile. 'I know it too. My wife's busy doing hers in your second reception room.'

Diane's jaw dropped. 'You mean . . .?'

'I mean DC Caroline Jackson is my wife.' He followed Mitchell to the kitchen and Diane, defeated, went back to her guests.

Someone had cleared the bottles from the table. When Cavill went to sit at it, Mitchell was careful to place his own chair beside rather than opposite him, waving away the uniformed constable who appeared in the doorway. He grinned at Cavill, trying to dissipate his antagonism. 'If you will keep on turning up on my bloody patch you must expect to be used.' When Cavill nodded, he continued, 'My notebook's out because you've spent a whole evening with these folk. I can't hold all you tell me in my head when their names mean nothing to me. What are they like and what the hell are you doing here?'

Now Cavill grinned widely. 'I've come on a lot of tickets. I was invited because Diane Bates got the idea that I was famous.'

'You are. Renowned, she called you.'

'Yes. She asked me to play the piano to entertain at the do here – what she called the reception. When I refused, I wondered if I'd be uninvited – but that would have been unladylike. Anyway, knowing me isn't going to do her any favours in her circle. Then, I'm the church organist so I was lumped together with the vicar.'

'OK, that's why she invited you. You haven't given me a reason yet why you showed up.'

'Because I liked Edgar and I liked Lorraine.'

'You knew them?' Cavill saw no need to answer this. 'How did you meet them?'

'Edgar tootled his horn in the senior cits' orchestra. He wasn't too bad at it either.'

'Was Lorraine a musician?'

'Not that I know of, but she was fond of Edgar, fetched him from rehearsals if the weather was bad and always suffered the concerts.'

'Then I'm sorry that you've lost two friends. What can you tell me about the rest?'

Cavill scratched his head. 'It's a crazily complicated family and I have one more slight connection with it. Lorraine's son, Philip, is engaged. The girl's father is head of Victor Grant's. In fact, he is Victor Grant.'

'Rich connections?'

'He's chief sponsor of the old dears' orchestra and pours money into it so long as I keep his name prominent in the programmes.'

'And mention him when the *Clarion* sends its reporters along? OK. What about your champion, the lady whose premises we're on?'

'I'd never met her till we made the funeral arrangements. She rang up and told me when she was coming. I said I'd be giving a recital in France that day and offered the phone number of my deputy.'

'I don't suppose he would do.'

'He'd have done very well but she wasn't having him. She became very gracious – said we must arrange a time to suit me and she would allow me to advise her about everything.'

'Big of her.'

'I couldn't believe she was Lorraine's sister. St Barnabas' isn't her church but she said it was the one Edgar attended.

I didn't disagree. It was certainly the church he attended for orchestra rehearsals. Anyway, both sisters came along, though I felt Lorraine wasn't welcome. She wanted to give Edgar what she called a good send-off. Diane kept talking about the dignity due to their father. She curled her lip at the new prayer book and demanded the "proper" one.'

'Did she give you a free hand with the music?'

He nodded. 'I told her Edgar liked Purcell.' Now Cavill was laughing. 'I told her the setting I had in mind had been composed for the funeral of Queen Mary. I realized after a bit that she understood this to mean the wife of George V, rather than the Tudor daughter of Henry VIII. I described how no expense had been spared, the road to Westminster being lined with black railings and a procession of three hundred women in black capes with young boys carrying their trains. She just said, "I expect Edgar remembered that – saw it on the films, you know."'

Chapter Three

Detective Constable Adrian Clement locked his door behind him. He had finished his stretches and he continued his warm-up with a brisk jog along the road. When he felt he was moving easily, he began to stride out and had soon completed a couple of six-minute miles. He was sweating gently and beginning to enjoy himself.

This was a good time of day to be out. Villains preferred the very early hours just after midnight. People moving around at five o'clock – and there were not many of them – were generally going about their lawful business. There were hardly any cars to fill his lungs with petrol or diesel fumes, or to hold him up and break his rhythm when his route crossed a main road.

Clement exulted in his sense of waiting for the day to begin. In another half-hour at the most it would be full daylight and then the peace and promise would be gone.

A big ginger cat almost tripped him and he could just make out its shape, slinking guiltily away along the bottom of a wall – or maybe it was stalking away, offended by Clement's feet in its path. The magic was disappearing already. Birds were calling to each other and Clement wished he could identify the different species. One he did recognize was a crow, perched on a branch and addressing him angrily for disturbing its morning routine.

He glanced at his watch before slowing down to the fast walk that began his warm-down. Sixty-five minutes for the eleven and a bit miles – his usual standard but no better. He hoped that he was not reaching the peak of his potential yet. There were still races that he intended to win.

His cell phone rang. He listened carefully to Mitchell's message, then abandoned his warm-down and made all speed for home. Hardly time even for a shower before leaping into his car.

By seven o'clock he was parking outside number 8 Elm Road. He could see his CI's venerable Cavalier at the top of the wide gravelled drive but decided to leave his Fiesta on the street.

Approaching it on foot, he walked round the house, examining it with interest. At the front, the white paint gleamed against the yellow sandstone and the lawns and flower beds gave the impression of being the work of a professional. At the back, all was just as clean and tidy, but the woodwork was peeling slightly and the back lawn showed a less than proficient attempt to copy the expert stripes achieved at the front.

Clement made mental notes before climbing the two steps to the door and pressing a bell in a well-polished brass surround. He was surprised when DC Caroline Jackson opened the door to him, and shocked at her appearance. Her athletic frame drooped and her scar stood out, livid on the white skin of her cheek. His feelings were mixed. He resented her having been called to this incident several hours earlier than himself, but he was fond of Caroline and concerned. Because she was female, and because, some time ago, he had unsuccessfully offered himself as a suitor, to express his concern was taboo, and he asked, merely, 'Have you been here all night? Why didn't you call me?'

Caroline closed the door behind him. 'You'd just finished a seventeen-hour day. We wouldn't have got much done with all of us half asleep. Now you're here, I'll put you in the picture and then snatch a couple of hours. The team is meeting in the CI's office at nine thirty. Anyway, we've spent the night with four extremely efficient PCs. The boss wants to hang on to them if he can.'

Mitchell appeared in the doorway. Succinctly he gave

Clement all the information he had collected about Lorraine Felling and her death, including the chief points of his interview with Neville Scott. Clement grinned at the doctor's caveat concerning Donna's evidence.

'Is he afraid that her stories will hold up the enquiry – or is he covering himself, afraid that she'll say something about him that he doesn't want us to know?'

'We'll perhaps have a better idea when we've spoken to her. At the moment she's asleep, or at least in bed, at the Granby Arms, in the care of her aunt and uncle who live here.'

Clement raised an eyebrow. 'The Granby? They aren't without a penny or two then.' So why, he wondered, the peeling paint? 'Why isn't the girl with her father?'

Mitchell stifled a yawn. 'Ask him yourself. I'd like you to see him as soon as possible. From my own brief acquaintance with the family, I'd say he was the one we're likely to find the most co-operative. I'd also like you to have a word with the sister and her husband.'

Clement wrote down Nicholas Felling's address in his notebook. 'SOCO still upstairs?' Mitchell nodded. 'Where's the body?'

'Safe with the Coroner's Officer. Ray's doing the PM at ten thirty. Apparently Felling's a schoolmaster. He probably won't be going into school today but you'd better get round early in case he is.'

'What do I want from him?'

Mitchell closed his eyes briefly to consider and Clement wondered if he would be able to open them again. 'An all-round view of the victim and the family situation and then anything he's prepared to volunteer. Right, let's go.'

He refused Clement's offer to drive him home. 'Just make sure you catch Felling before he leaves. He looks the conscientious type who would stagger into work, come what may.'

Clement could hardly believe his luck. Mitchell, on this first morning of a new case, was snatching some well-earned and much-needed sleep. Sergeant Taylor, his CI's trusty deputy, was safe in court this morning. As he wandered down the drive to his car, Clement willed her case to drag on all day. This was his chance to make a head start and some startling discoveries. It was high time that he was promoted to sergeant himself. Getting out his town plan of Cloughton, he studied it. He thought he knew the run-down street where Felling apparently lived, but he'd better check. It didn't strike him as a likely choice for a teacher.

It was barely a quarter past seven when Clement turned into Victoria Road, but he imagined that Felling would hardly have slept long or well and would probably be up. He noticed that at least some of the houses seemed in better fettle than was the case the last time he had driven past them. The trees too looked less vandalized and healthier. Perhaps the district was on its way up again. If so he was glad. He had been irritated to see this fine Victorian terrace disintegrating.

Number 16 had its woodwork freshly painted. Outside it were parked a gleaming motor bike, a Mini van and a dilapidated Renault 4. A row of labelled bells told him his quarry lived in one of the attic rooms on the second floor. He appeared so immediately after Clement pressed the bell that the DC wondered if he had taken each flight of stairs at one leap. Clad in jeans and a short dressing gown, Felling blinked at the ID he was offered, then stood back to let his visitor in.

'Were you expecting someone else?' Clement asked, amused.

Felling nodded. 'I thought it might be someone bringing my daughter back. I don't expect her to last long with the Bateses before there's a falling out. She ought to be with me anyway, but the doctor gave her a sedative last night, and, as Diane pointed out, the hotel is more comfortable than here.'

Clement was close behind him as he began on the second flight of stairs, observing the athletic stride. Felling indicated with a movement of his head that the DC should follow him through the door he had left ajar. 'We'd better be quiet. The rest of the house sleeps in till about eight.'

41

Clement made a swift appraisal of the room he had entered. It was clean and bare, uncarpeted except for a rug beside the narrow divan in the corner. The stretches of white-painted walls were relieved only by bookcases, and cooking facilities were represented by a gas ring and an ancient toaster on a plastic-topped table. The door opposite, slightly open, revealed a modern lavatory and shower cubicle.

Felling waved an arm, offering his living quarters to Clement's less than tactful inspection. 'No luxuries but all the necessities – at least, all that was necessary for me. It won't be enough now I'm having Donna with me.'

Clement was surprised. 'You have just the one room? You don't live with your daughter and your partner?'

Felling grinned ruefully. 'Not for some time.' As Clement sought for the least offensive way to get him to elaborate, he offered, 'Shall I give you the family tree and where we all fit in?' Clement nodded gratefully. 'I'll start at the beginning then and tell you all I've time for.'

'You're going into school today?'

'No chance, but Diane's going to ring as soon as Donna wakes and then I shall have to go to her.' Clement indicated his agreement to this proviso.

Felling filled the kettle and set it on the lighted gas ring before beginning his account. 'Edgar – whose funeral it was – and May had two girls. Lorraine was the wild child. Diane was the respectable one, doing well at school, getting a job in a bank, marrying her boss and living a luxurious life in her posh house.'

'So the Bateses' money is from banking?'

'He's manager of Barclay's in Silver Street – the main branch.'

'Right. Go on with your relationships.'

'Lorraine was bright too, in her own way, but not academic. I sometimes wonder if she got pregnant partly to get out of doing A-levels. Anyway, having incurred responsibility for him, she kept Philip by doing a series of jobs her relations considered "not quite suitable", things

42

she could do when the baby was in bed, such as bar work and cleaning.'

'She got married, didn't she? Was it to the child's father?'

'No. He went off to university and was never seen again. His parents moved away too. She met her husband much later. Lorraine loved Mark and he adopted the child. He's Philip Conroy, not Smith. Lorraine was only married to Mark for two years and then he was killed in a car smash.'

'And then you came on the scene?'

'Well, yes. I kept a low profile till she'd got over things a bit. It didn't take too long. Lorraine had a very buoyant personality. She'd loved Mark very much but . . .'

His voice broke and he paused, then shrugged and continued his narrative briskly. 'We lasted four years, Lorraine and I. She moved in with me – not here, of course – and Donna was born the year after. She wasn't a mistake,' he declared defensively. 'We both love her dearly. When we broke up, custody of Donna was the only thing we argued about.' He turned away and began preparing a makeshift breakfast, perhaps as a way of leaving the subject of his break away from his partner.

Felling's mood seemed to have changed. 'You'll want to know about yesterday.'

At this stage, Clement wanted whatever was available to him. His 'Please' was a comprehensive acceptance of the information and the mimed offer of a share of the breakfast that was in preparation.

Felling turned his back again to pour tea. 'You've obviously been told I'm a teacher.'

Clement nodded. In any case, he would have worked out for himself that the man's work was in communicating ideas and opinions, and he hoped that the clearly tabulated information he was receiving and noting would reflect some credit on himself.

Felling continued his recital. 'To get time off, I had to claim that Edgar was my father-in-law. In my eyes, that's just what he was. I'd have married Lorraine with no hesitation if she'd agreed to it, though whether I'd have been as happy to take on the Bateses as my in-laws is another question. Anyway, there was no wedding, so, in Diane's eyes, I wasn't family and wasn't included in the official arrangements. I arrived in my own car, the clapped-out Renault outside.'

Felling handed Clement a plate of buttered toast and they ate, facing each other across the tiny table. He drank half his tea while making up his mind to it, then announced, 'You might as well know sooner than later that Lorraine had a drink problem. When I first arrived, I pushed my way to the kitchen and found her in there, filling her glass, probably not for the first time. She gave me a peck on the cheek, then went into the sitting room. I followed her, slowly because it was crowded. I blessed Barry. I think he realized what was going on. I saw him coming out of the kitchen just after me with a tray of full bottles. He took them down to the cellar.

'I thought Barry himself looked a bit out of sorts towards the end – a bit under the weather. I thought he might have had a tipple too many himself. He's a very good host usually – rounds up the misfits at Diane's parties and looks after them. He'd spent quite a time, for instance, talking, or rather, listening to old Walter Denby and getting him comfortably settled, but he didn't look in much better shape himself. He went through to sit in the conservatory at the back of the house for a while.'

Felling stopped to put more bread in the toaster, then took a deep breath as though coming to the part of his narration that was unpleasant to him. 'I followed Lorraine into the big sitting room on the right of the stairs. She was putting a CD into Diane's complicated hi-fi system. It was something out of the pop charts and a lot of the guests were disapproving. There was a lot of tutting, but, once they'd started on the mountain of food in the dining room and the drink was flowing, someone turned the music up. I think the CD must have been Donna's. It wasn't the sort of thing Diane would buy.

'There was enough alcohol in the kitchen to float a liner.

I don't know whether Diane was being spiteful or just thoughtless. The whole affair was like a macabre birthday party in a house decorated with sympathy cards in white and silver and tall white vases filled with tall white lilies to match.'

'I bet you teach English literature.'

Felling blinked. 'I do, actually. Sorry.'

'Go on with your story.'

Felling's lips tightened. 'I heard someone behind me saying things would liven up soon when Lorraine got legless. Actually, I thought it was a good thing she couldn't take her liquor. It usually bit her back before she'd taken enough on board to rot her liver or completely poison her system. I knew from long experience that there was nothing I could do to stop her, so I joined the food queue.'

'Was it the drinking that split you up?'

Felling shook his head. 'It wasn't this bad when we were together. I can't put my finger on what it was. Philip was very difficult. Lorraine was afraid that I resented his being with us but I didn't. I'm not saying he didn't drive us both to distraction on occasion but I could understand that. He was passed round the family when he was tiny while Lorraine was at work. Then he settled down with Mark and as soon as he'd begun to feel secure, Mark had his accident. Philip had given up trusting life to give him a fair deal by the time I came on the scene. He was just eleven when Donna arrived, quite the wrong age for a lad to want a baby around. Lorraine's pregnancy embarrassed him too. But maybe he has learned to trust now. At least, he's got himself engaged.

'It wasn't Philip who got between us, though. Lorraine didn't trust life either. She was always high-spirited, cheerful in a brittle sort of way, but not quite happy, never peacefully content.'

Felling paused to control his quivering lower lip and the telephone rang. Hoping he had gathered as much information as his DCI required for the moment, Clement gathered his possessions and allowed Felling, whose dressing gown had been replaced by a sweatshirt, to usher him out.

The telephone message had been brief. Felling had spoken only two words to his caller, 'Right. Thanks,' and to his visitor, 'Donna's awake.' He took the two flights of stairs three at a time and, when Clement reached the pavement, he was seated in the Renault which was emitting stertorous grunts from beneath the bonnet and evil-smelling black smoke from the exhaust.

Clement was pleased. It would have been awkward to have followed Felling to the hotel. Now he could offer him a lift. Felling leapt into the Fiesta with perfunctory thanks and climbed out at the hotel entrance without even that. Clement had seen the pointlessness of continued questioning and had remained silent throughout the short journey.

As both men followed the receptionist's pointing finger to the dining room, Clement saw Mr and Mrs Bates and their niece seated at a breakfast table in the corner. The young girl half smiled at her father as he slid into the empty chair beside her. Then she played with a finger of toast, her eyes seemingly on her plate and her long fair hair in two curtains that hid her face.

Reminded by Diane Bates, Felling remembered his manners, beckoning Clement forward to introduce him. Before he could reply, Mrs Bates drew him aside, standing so abruptly to do so that her husband had to catch her chair to stop it overturning. 'Good morning, constable. We have an important discovery to report.'

Clement sighed. It seemed that Lorraine and Donna were not the only people in this case who loved striking poses. For Barry Bates the discovery, whatever it was, did not rate equal in importance with coaxing his niece to eat some of her toast. Unabashed, Diane continued. 'I'm afraid we were robbed yesterday afternoon.'

Clement blinked. 'Robbed? You didn't say anything about it last night, did you? Still, I suppose that's understandable in all the circumstances . . .'

'Of course, I noticed things were missing yesterday but I thought Barry had taken them away.'

'Your husband? Why should he do that?'

46

'Well, we thought things might get – a little out of hand, shall we say?'

'You mean that with so much alcohol in the house you thought that your sister would get drunk and your possessions might be damaged?'

Clement watched the woman trying to decide against which of his inferences to defend herself first. 'I can't deny my guests a drink just because my sister –'

'I presume,' Clement cut in, 'you have since discovered that Mr Bates did not take the precautions you anticipated and you have concluded your possessions have been stolen.' She nodded. 'So, what's missing?'

'My Fabergé egg from the bookcase and my George III bracket clock from the mantelpiece.' She appealed to him piteously, 'We'll have to go back home and make a list. I only noticed the house looked bare but I didn't worry because I thought the things were safe and I had so much else on my mind.' She waved a hand to indicate the range of yesterday's worries. 'The catering, the flowers, trying to keep an eye on Lorraine . . .'

'Not to mention your two bereavements.'

She flushed angrily and Clement was ashamed of himself. He glanced back at the table in the corner and saw that Felling had prevailed on his daughter to eat her toast. She had pushed her hair back behind her ears and he saw the likeness between father and daughter, the clear olive complexion in startling combination with fair hair and blue eyes, hers inky and his almost grey.

They all turned as they heard new voices and Clement saw a young couple standing in the doorway. The man was the epitome of a young executive in dark suit, white shirt and soberly patterned tie. His short dark hair had been disciplined and he regarded Clement quizzically through fashionable spectacles with black wire frames.

The girl was an altogether suitable companion for him in a blackberry-coloured suit and a wide-brimmed hat of woven straw pulled low over her face. She was attractive in a sharp sort of way. Clement thought the thin features would have been painted to advantage if she had stopped

47

marginally sooner. Perhaps the heavy make-up was deliberate, though. There seemed to be some sort of disfigurement on the cheek now turned away from him.

'Philip!' His aunt seemed delighted to see him. 'And Toni. Come and sit down, dear, and have some coffee. That's a very fetching hat.'

Philip addressed Diane. 'We've only popped in to see how you all are. Then Toni's driving to the airport to pick up her father.'

The girl came forward and turned towards the light. 'I've chosen this hat to hide my face.' She raised it and they examined and exclaimed over the scratches she displayed on her forehead and cheek. 'Bonkers threw me into a bank of brambles,' she explained briefly.

In the momentary surprised silence that followed, Clement stepped forward and Felling hastily introduced Lorraine's son and his fiancée. The DC's nod took in the whole family as he apologized for questioning them when they were still shocked and upset. He singled out the Bateses with a further nod. 'Perhaps we could go up to your room while I ask you for some details about yesterday afternoon.'

Out of the corner of his eye, Clement was still watching the rest of the party. The half brother and sister were obviously on good terms. Philip tugged at Donna's long hair and slid into the chair beside her that Barry Bates had vacated. Felling too seemed pleased to see the young man. Donna was not so welcoming to his companion. She scowled as the young woman settled down on the far side of her brother and appropriated his attention.

Diane Bates was reluctant to accompany her husband upstairs. 'I thought we were going back to the house to make a list of what's missing.' She answered the questioning glances of the newcomers with a renewed recital of her woes.

Clement ran out of patience. 'Mrs Bates, which matter would you prefer me to concentrate on, finding your sister's killer or finding who stole your knick-knacks?' Diane's mouth hardened and Clement wondered whether she was annoyed by the renewal of his implied criticism of her lack of feeling or by his disrespectful manner of referring to her valuable possessions.

From the table, Philip addressed him for the first time. 'If you've found one, you might well have found the other.'

Diane beamed. 'Well, of course. Otherwise I wouldn't be making a fuss about the missing things.'

Clement firmly closed his lips and shepherded his interviewees to their room. Once he had got her embarked on her account of the previous day, Diane was free with her opinions and observations. She had been surprised that Nicholas had decided to come to the funeral. He was not part of the family, of course, but she had been pleased to see him as an insurance policy. He had become quite adept at dealing quietly and tactfully with her sister's excesses. She suspected he had come along more with the purpose of meeting Lorraine again – and Donna, of course – than as a tribute to Edgar.

She had noticed early on that one of her treasures was not in its usual place, the bracket clock from the mantelpiece. Barry had told her earlier that he had intended to lock a few things away before her sister began smashing the place up. She had thought he was joking then, but later she had supposed he was serious.

Barry Bates confirmed each of his wife's sentences with a nod. Clement found it difficult to believe he had made such a positive suggestion and decided it had probably been Diane's own. Perched on the end of the bed, she was in full flow and enjoying herself. 'Otherwise, all things considered, I was pleased with how things were going. Lorraine's music, if music it could be called, ruined the whole tone, of course, but she'd done worse on past occasions and it could be borne.'

'Everyone would have known that Diane was not responsible.'

Clement blinked at Barry's brief interruption and this time it was his wife who nodded assent.

'Yes, I really thought I could relax at that stage and allow myself a small slice of the chocolate gateau. It gave me a chance to check that those two giggling women were clearing up properly, putting leftover food in the fridge and freezer and not helping themselves.'

'You had professional caterers for the occasion?'

'Of course. How could I concentrate on the church service if I had the feeding of fifty guests to worry about?'

Clement asked for details of the chosen company and Diane cheered up. 'You might well find your villain there, I'm afraid, but you can hardly ask everyone who washed up or carried a tray of drinks to be police vetted.'

Clement asked ironically, 'And was all well – when you checked up on them?'

'Reasonably. I was distracted by Donna. She was burrowing under the sofa cushions with her hands for something she'd lost. I thought how attractive she was getting. Watching her, I half regretted that I'd never had a daughter of my own. Whatever she was looking for, she didn't find it, and when she saw I was looking at her she left the room. They're so gauche at that age, aren't they?'

Giving his witness her head was not producing the information he required, and Clement resorted to direct questions. 'What was your sister doing all this time?'

Diane shrugged apologetically. 'I hadn't noticed the state Lorraine had got herself into till I saw Nick and Philip taking her upstairs. She was babbling to herself. I called up to them that the spare bed was made up.' She tutted. 'Nick had no more sense than to cover her with my lace spread. I hope to goodness the cleaners will be able to deal with it.' She noticed Clement's expression. 'Not that that's the most important thing in the circumstances, of course.'

'Of course. So, what happened next?'

'They came down. Nick complimented me on a well-run reception. I was surprised. He's usually rather aloof with me. I asked if he thought they'd all like coffee before they left and I went into the kitchen to do it. The hired women had gone by then. Philip helped me and Mrs Wayman from next door. Nick offered too, but I got him to go and replace the dance music with something more in keeping with the occasion. He chose a Bach organ prelude, much more fitting.'

Clement nodded. 'I understand you went up to the bedroom your sister was using.'

Diane closed her eyes and swallowed. 'I needed some extra trays to take the coffee round. I went up and saw that – well, Lorraine was ill. I was a bit worried about her and I went down and asked Neville if he'd pop in and have a look at her. I never realized she was . . .'

As the painted face he was watching disintegrated, Clement saw that Diane was now genuinely upset. His tone was less harsh as he asked, 'You didn't realize that she was dead?'

She sniffed and smeared mascara over her cheeks with another lace-edged handkerchief. 'Not till Neville came downstairs. He stood at the bottom and there was something about his manner that made us all turn to him and be quiet. He just said he was sorry to have to tell us . . .' Sobs drowned her words.

Barry Bates had made no move to comfort his wife. He continued to stand and nod. Clement wondered what he would have to say for himself in a one-to-one interview but a glance at his watch told him that there was no time for it now. He had ten minutes to get himself to his DCI's briefing.

Leaving his lady of the moment to paint and deck herself into a fit state to appear in the hotel dining room for breakfast, Victor Grant entered the en-suite bathroom she had just vacated. He wrinkled his nose at the heavy musky mix of perfumes she had left behind there and opened the window before beginning his own grooming for the day. He stood under an efficient shower, removing the heat and sweat of his nocturnal activities, and tried to calculate the time his wife would be expecting him to arrive home if he had returned from Hanover on this morning's flight as she thought he had.

The plane that his obliging colleague had taken in his

place should touch down at ten thirty-five. If he allowed twenty minutes to retrieve his suitcase and another fifteen for a quick coffee . . .? His exertions seemed to have addled his brain. It should be all right if he was ready to leave this hotel at about ten. If he was held up on the road, his excuse would be genuine and Glenda could check with the traffic police if she liked. Splendid. He'd better ring the airport, though, to make sure the flight arrived on time.

He grimaced in irritation as he realized that Karen had used both bath sheets, so that he had to dry himself on the remaining hand towels. Then, disdaining the aftershave and cologne provided by the hotel, he used his own. He and Karen wouldn't go downstairs, he decided. He'd send for a tray and they'd eat up here. That should leave an hour or two for more sexual gymnastics. He returned to his opulent bedroom.

Karen's repeat performance was disappointing and Victor was ready to leave for home in advance of his plan. It had been a sticky moment when Toni had rung his mobile this morning and offered to meet him at the airport. He didn't like telling off-the-cuff lies. If they weren't carefully planned they caught you out. Toni gave him the news of Lorraine's death and she seemed a bit fazed by it herself. There was something about her tone when she gave him the news. It hinted at her suspicion that he and Lorraine had a relationship a bit closer than the tenuous one that would be created when his daughter married her son – if she ever got round to it.

Things could have become very awkward. Lorraine had turned out to be less manageable, less easy to sweep off her feet than he had anticipated. Her family was used to her odd liaisons and their inconvenient results, but he was on his last chance with Glenda.

Chapter Four

As the team gathered in the incident room, Detective Superintendent John Carroll was returning to Cloughton, anxious to oversee the current investigation as Mitchell expected – maybe feared. Mitchell's description of his superintendent's role substituted 'hobble' for 'oversee'.

Whichever was the apposite term, Carroll was now climbing into Commander Wren's gleaming, dark green BMW with less enthusiasm than when they had set out together three days ago. The course they had attended was not the reason for his apprehension. It had been billed as 'Time of Death' and had not been quite what they had expected. This was due, not in small part, to two lectures delivered on the first day by his own area's newly appointed pathologist. Ray Holland had spoken in informative and entertaining fashion on the history of forensic science as it related to the course title.

Carroll felt little guilt at having left his patch for three days, even though the time had proved more diverting than useful. His discomfiture was caused by the commander's diabolical driving and the fact that DCI Benedict Mitchell had begun an investigation into a suspicious death without his own restraining supervision. He was now hoping for the best on two counts.

He trusted his CI absolutely to find his man, knew he liked 'nicking people'. He had given telephoned permission for him to take charge. Surely he wouldn't create much mayhem in one morning . . .

The car jerked out of the conference centre drive and on to the road into a too-narrow gap between a decrepit

Bedford van and a shiny new Celica. Carroll tried to decide whether his best plan as a passenger was to talk or remain silent. On the whole, talking worked better. The commander seemed to listen with his eyes on the road but turned to face him when he had anything to say. Experimentally, he remarked on his going home to what might prove to be a new murder case.

The commander grunted. 'So, what's your DCI like?'

'Flippant and disrespectful. On the ball. Local – knows his patch and people. He plays a case like he plays a game of rugby, light-hearted and enjoying the exercise but determined to win.' Carroll averted his eyes from the bumper of the vehicle just a yard in front and rushed on nervously. 'The sixteenth century as Dr Holland described it would have been a good period for him, provoking suspects to get a confession, provided that a hatchet man or lynchman hadn't dispatched the accused before he made it behind bars.'

The commander was eager to show that he too had paid attention to the lecture. 'We've the Declaration of the Rights of Man and the French Revolution to thank for our "Innocent till proven . . ."' He broke off and deigned to return his attention to the road in response to a blast from the horn of the car behind. 'So, what's your chap's problem?'

'He doesn't think he's got one. He's just a maverick. Gets his results by breaking the rules – not of decency, just bureaucracy. He hasn't much patience, though my other DCI has missed chances through caution. I have to be prepared to mop up Benny's spills, or get someone else to.'

'Sounds more trouble than he's worth.'

'Yes and no. Together we get the job done.' Carroll was silent for a few moments as he wondered how his companion could so abuse this beautiful car, stabbing at the accelerator so that they constantly jerked forward and slamming through the gearbox. He began to worry about a third problem and tried to apply mind over matter as a way of controlling his stomach.

'What you're actually saying is that you like him.'

'True. So do his men – well, actually, all but one of his team are women.'

'I see.'

'No, you don't. His wife can match any of them for brains and the rest. Not that Ginny is beautiful in any classical sense but she sparkles so you don't notice the details that don't measure up.'

'Ha! You're keeping in with him to keep in with her!' Triumphantly he beat the car alongside him on to a roundabout.

Carroll swallowed. 'Fat chance. She's twenty-something.'

'So how old's your saintly DCI?'

'Too old for her, probably. He's thirty-seven.' Suddenly, it occurred to Carroll that this man might have Mitchell's preferment in his gift. He remained silent for a while, thinking over their conversation and hoping he had done his DCI no disservice.

He was roused from his reverie by a loud shout. 'You bloody fool!' Thankfully, he realized this was only the commander's response to some caustic criticism from another driver. During the unedifying exchange that followed, while both drivers' vehicles continued to travel forward, Carroll prayed for all road users, but especially for those on the M62 that morning.

Fifteen minutes later, he was dropped off at headquarters. After offering insincere thanks, he retired thankfully to his own office until his stomach and spirits should have recovered from the journey sufficiently for him to deal with the further trials Mitchell would provide for him.

Something less than two hours' sleep seemed to have restored Mitchell's habitual alert expression. 'This briefing really will be brief,' he told them. 'I'm due at the PM in less than an hour. Once we officially have a murder there's a chance we'll have adequate manpower.'

Since all the other three officers had been asleep since leaving Elm Road, Clement was invited to report on his preliminary findings. He described his aborted interview with Nicholas Felling and Diane Bates's account of the reception at her house, including the burglary that had presumably occurred during the funeral service itself. 'I sent for a car and Smithson is helping them make a list of what's missing. Philip Conroy and his girlfriend have gone to work but will make themselves available as required. Mr Felling is taking his daughter home – to his bedsitter, that is.'

'Where does she usually live?'

'With her mother in Mr Felling's house in Maybridge. When I said we'd be looking at it, he gave me his key. I expect we've got Lorraine's but I brought this one anyway. Whenever we ring him, he'll come in to finish his account and sign his statement.'

'So, what did you make of them all?'

Clement considered. 'I like Felling. He seems a straightforward sort of chap.'

'You didn't take to Mrs Bates?'

Clement shrugged. 'She's just a middle-aged woman, well off with no children. She centres her life round her possessions. I've nothing in common with her but not much against her. I'd just decided she didn't give a toss about losing her sister when it suddenly seemed to hit her. I liked her better after that. By the way, she referred to the stolen goods as "my loss" rather than "ours". And, another funny thing – their two lists, his and hers, of what had been taken didn't match. Diane Bates's list was longer. I've marked the items that aren't common to both. It's all in the file.'

One of the four borrowed PCs was looking puzzled. 'Do we need to see all these people, sir, now we know about the burglar? Shouldn't we be looking for him?'

'We are looking for him, or at least, we shall be as soon as Superintendent Carroll gives me some more people. In the meantime we'll talk to the victim's immediate relatives and friends.'

'But don't you think . . .?' The PC heeded the DCI's warning look and ground to a halt.

Mitchell said patiently, 'Beardsmore, is it? Yes, I think it's

56

quite likely the chap was trapped in the house with the loot about his person. He may have disturbed Lorraine and used a pillow to stop her yelling, possibly not meaning to kill her. Even if that's so, we need to know what the Bateses' guests saw. Any more ideas?'

The PC opened his mouth, then shut it again. When they all turned to him, he merely shook his head.

Mitchell grinned at him. 'I won't eat you.' Still there was no comment forthcoming and Mitchell went on, 'Right, time for the lab. Beardsmore, you haven't seen a PM yet, have you? You'd better come to this one. Adrian, you can go back to Elm Road and set them looking for signs of a break-in. Have a look at that spare bedroom now forensic have finished with it and have a quick scan round the rest of the house. We'll compare notes later. If you're going to see Felling again, get him to leave the girl somewhere else. I want to be there for her. Take Shakila with you. Oh, and Smithson!' The elderly PC looked up, pencil poised. 'Get the details of the Bateses' catering firm from Adrian. Have a word with all the staff they sent to the house. They were doubtless run off their feet, but what they did notice they'll be ready to tell.'

The team of white-overalled scene of crime officers were unperturbed when Clement and Shakila presented them with a new set of circumstances that included breaking and entering. As one of them expressed it, 'We look for what there is to find, not what there is to support the latest theory.' The three men searching the garden had already discovered the splintering around the lock of the heavy door to the semi-basement. Both officers surveyed it from a carefully designated patch of concrete path on which they were allowed to stand. The door looked formidable but the SOCO demonstrated that the wood was soft and damp.

It was an ideal spot from which to break in unseen. It was reached by half a dozen stone steps leading down from the level of the garden, away from the house windows and screened from the house next door by large shrubs. The garden was huge, its privacy protected by tall beech hedges, now in their golden-brown autumn glory.

The Bateses and their accompanying officer had already returned to their hotel, having eventually agreed that less than a dozen smallish objects had been stolen, carefully chosen for their value and portability. They had included two pictures: the absence of one was marked by a small unfaded oblong on the cream wallpaper in the drawing room.

The areas still unexamined, which Clement and Shakila were not allowed to sully, did not include the staircase, the landing or the room in which Lorraine's body had been lying. This room was carefully decorated in the same style as the rest of the house, but it had the feel of all spare rooms, being a repository for all the objects not immediately required in the rest of the house but too good or useful to throw away. It had taken nothing from the personalities of its users. There was a just-discernible pale patch on a wall here too.

Clement regarded it. 'Did the thief make a mistake here? Diane wouldn't hang a picture worth stealing in a room she didn't use.'

Shakila had been dismissed to her bed the previous night much earlier than Caroline and was well up to arguing with Clement in her usual fashion. She turned from admiring the view of the garden. 'She would if she liked impressing people. This is where she put her visitors.'

Clement nodded approvingly. 'OK. If this picture being missing means that the burglar was in here, what do we think happened? He could have darted into the cloakroom when he heard voices, then come out when it was quiet and been surprised to find Lorraine still here.'

'Or she could.'

'Yes, a woman could have done it just as easily, I suppose.'

The bed had obviously been thoroughly examined. The lace cover and the pillow that the killer had used had both been removed. As Clement turned the remaining bedding

58

over again a strong waft of cheap perfume was released and Shakila muttered to herself.

'What did you say?'

Shakila grinned. 'Californian Poppy. It really brings back my spotty teens. When I was about fifteen I used to spend my pocket money on it. I thought it was going to seduce the junior soccer captain and I went to school reeking of it if my brother didn't catch me and make me wash it off. I didn't expect to smell it in this house.'

'You're sure? About it being exactly that smell, I mean.'

'I'd know it anywhere. Wish I didn't.'

The two officers searched for a while longer but found only temporarily abandoned summer clothes in the drawers and wardrobe, together with spare bedding. The big break, they decided, would have to be found elsewhere.

Nicholas Felling was being treated, for the moment at least, as a co-operative witness rather than a suspect. Mitchell had therefore left instructions that Clement should use his office to talk to him rather than a fly-strewn, disinfectant-smelling interview room. When the fuss over the allocation of seating was over, Felling said uncertainly, 'I've forgotten where I'd got to.'

Clement shook his head. 'It doesn't matter. Just go on talking about yesterday in whatever order things occur to you. Tell me what you thought about everything as well as what happened.'

Felling nodded his understanding of what was required. 'The door was opened to me by a stranger and the hall was filled with people I didn't know. That seemed strange when we were all paying our respects to the same man. It shows what wide interests he had.'

'It also shows how difficult this investigation is going to be. No one will be able to tell us whether they saw anyone who had no right to be there.'

Felling shrugged. 'All right. I saw Lorraine talking to a pompous little man. I know now it was Neville Scott. He was paying close attention to what she was saying and he seemed incongruous company for her. I was curious so I wandered over to them. She introduced us. She was trying to shock him rather than upset me, I think. She said, "Neville, this is Nicholas Felling, my ex, the one who isn't defunct."'

'Did she upset you?'

He smiled. 'No more than usual. Then they talked about the dramatic society they both belonged to. I wasn't very interested so I "circulated" some more, as Diane had asked us to. I had a quick word with Donna but Diane had her busy helping and she was bustling about, quite enjoying herself in a suitably restrained way. Not that she hadn't been very fond of her grandfather. We all were.

'Later, Lorraine was dancing to the music she'd put on the CD player and I started talking to Philip. Then the commotion broke out.'

'Where?'

'In the dining room. I pushed through to the middle of it and found Lorraine crumpled on the floor as I'd expected. A young man had been dancing with her and he was looking down at her nonplussed. I'd never seen him before. Philip had followed me and we hauled Lorraine to her feet and hustled her out of sight and upstairs.'

'Did anyone else help?'

'Only by tactfully ignoring us. Diane hovered. Lorraine's public disgrace always half disgusted and half fascinated her. She shouted after us, "For God's sake don't put her on our bed,"' and we took her to the spare room, where we'd been going anyway.'

'Diane said Lorraine was – babbling, I think the word was. Do you know what about?'

Felling shook his head. 'I was behind her on the stairs but Philip said she was claiming to have a new job. He told me not to count on being a kept man because the first time they found her drunk they'd sack her.'

Clement winced. 'How do you get on with Philip?'

Felling paused to consider. 'Quite well on the whole. He's a bit awkward with me because of the terrible time he gave us as an adolescent. I admire him. He had a very difficult childhood as I've explained and he's working hard now and doing well for himself.'

'What did you do when you came downstairs?'

Felling frowned. 'I know Lorraine died very suddenly and there will have to be an inquest, but do you really need all this detail?'

'Mr Felling, we've learned from hard experience to cater for the worst situation. If the coroner is satisfied about the cause of death, we'll be glad to destroy all PC Beardsmore's painstaking notes. If by any chance he isn't, we'd have lost the sharpness of first impressions if we hadn't proceeded as if there was a case to answer.'

Felling nodded and answered the DC's question but his manner had become more guarded. 'As I came down, I saw Diane leaning against that chest of drawers in the hall. She looked exhausted and I was sorry for her. I always am.'

'Why?'

'Oh, all kinds of reasons. She has this anxious, ingratiating expression. She was hot and tired and her hair was easing itself out of the elaborate curls that her hairdresser had imposed on it so expensively. And people call her a snob because she's abandoned the local accent but she's just trying to keep her end up. She's always afraid she'll drop back into it.

'Anyway, she'd finished showing off her beautiful home and wanted it to herself again. I was sure the rest of us were as eager to go as she was to be rid of us but no one liked to be the first to break things up. I suggested that coffee to speed us on our way would be a sufficient hint.'

'Yes, Diane told me about the coffee. Your offer of help was refused and you were sent to change the music.'

'That's right. I found a CD with a miserable-looking face on the cover and it turned out to be mournful organ music. Just the thing to send everybody home. If you've had all this from Diane, why do you want it from me?'

'I've noticed some quite interesting differences in your

accounts.' Clement did not go on to confide how much these small contradictions were amusing him. 'If you would finish your own story, just briefly?'

Felling sighed and, with patience wearing thin, completed his summary. 'I went to talk to Mr Denby.' He anticipated the next question. 'He was Edgar's old chess partner. They spent hours poring over the board. He's getting very frail. I was surprised when he told me he was an executor for Edgar's will. He's a beer man and he'd been plied with spirits. He was remarking rather loudly that there were going to be "ructions" when the family found out what was in the will. I was trying to get him off the subject when I saw Diane in the doorway watching us. She went off to fetch some trays she kept in the spare room to carry the coffee round.

'A minute or two later she came storming back. When she's angry we get the old voice and her true colours – and then, afterwards, she worries because she thinks she's let herself down. Well, she collared Philip and told him his disgusting mother had thrown up all over her pillows. I think she expected him to rush upstairs and start cleaning. If she did, she was unlucky. Then Neville Scott said he'd go upstairs and have a look at her.'

Felling pulled a wry face and Clement asked, 'Did that not please you?'

'I thought it meant that he was my successor and I asked Philip if they were living together. He explained about Scott being a doctor. It wasn't long before he came down again and told us Lorraine was dead.'

'How did –'

Suddenly, Felling was angry. 'How did we all react to the news? Well, I "reacted" quite strongly myself. Lorraine was my partner, the mother of my daughter. I didn't realize at the time that I was on spy duty.'

This was not the question Clement had been about to ask but he allowed Felling to continue without interruption.

Felling pulled himself up, took a deep breath. 'I hoped he was wrong. I wanted to go to her. I was angry when

Scott barred the way. I tried to push past him but he didn't budge and Philip took my arm.'

Clement knew it was time to stop. Somehow, he had lost Felling's goodwill. 'It's inevitable, Mr Felling, that what I have to ask you is upsetting. Thank you for what you've told me. The rest can wait for a while.'

'You're only doing your job?' The words were mocking but the man's manner was a little less aggressive. Clement forbore to remind him that his daughter would be subjected to the same treatment later in the day.

It had occurred to Mitchell, even when he was still on his way to the mortuary, that Dr Holland was maybe not the ideal man for a rookie constable to observe on his first experience of a post-mortem. He escorted his protégé into the gleaming, cavernous space where no fewer than six corpses, including Lorraine's, rested on scrubbed white trolley-benches, awaiting the less than tender ministrations of the pathologist, and noted the younger officer's bitten lip and wary expression.

In an attempt to calm him and warm the atmosphere, he asked him, 'What's your first name?'

Glad to be distracted, Beardsmore grinned ruefully. 'It's Oliver, sir, but that didn't go down too well on the mining estate in Castleford where I was brought up. I was nick-named Bob, after a Cas rugby player with the same surname, and fortunately it stuck.'

Dr Holland soon dissipated the small increase in Beardsmore's confidence. Eyeing the lad's discomfiture with some contempt, he began to lecture him. 'This laboratory is a haven, a refuge where hours disappear like minutes . . .'

His CI gave Beardsmore a nod. Out of the side of his mouth, he hissed, 'Don't listen to him.' Mitchell tried to remember the effect that the smell of the place had had on him when he first encountered it – a mixture of disinfectant and preservatives, dead bugs and raw pork past its prime. At least that's how it had seemed to him once proceedings began. They watched as Dr Holland made the first incision and the now-familiar odour spread around them.

Beardsmore lasted precisely thirty seconds. As he left the room at speed, Mitchell sighed and turned his attention to the body on the table.

The flow of unwelcome information continued from the pathologist. 'Fatal asphyxia has three stages . . .' His knife was slicing efficiently through flesh and muscle with a sound rather like Mitchell's barber made with the scissors when cutting the thickest hair on his crown. 'Congestion . . . confusion and convulsions . . .' Dr Holland lifted Lorraine's left eyelid and even Mitchell was revolted by the blood in the socket, the livid red staining on the eyeball and the hugely dilated pupil.

By now he had managed to edit out from his sensory impressions both the smell and most of the extraneous commentary. He supposed the white-coated woman taking notes was describing what she observed rather than what she heard.

Beardsmore re-entered. After a brief assessing glance, Mitchell deliberately ignored him. With luck, he would survive the rest of the exercise. Dr Holland's tone had become salacious. 'Consciousness lost, pupils dilated, then death with terminal vomiting.'

Beardsmore's had apparently not been terminal. He surprised Mitchell by asking, 'So, did it happen as you explained before?'

'Well, a lumpy pillow wouldn't mould itself so that it completely closed the mouth and nostrils. However, the obstruction will increase as congestion develops and fluids pour into the mouth.'

Mitchell ventured a question of his own. 'I don't know how much it would help us or how accurate it's possible to be about the first couple of hours, but if you could establish a time of death within that . . .?'

He blinked as, with the knife still making its slicing noise, Dr Holland turned his head to answer. 'Just been lecturing on that very thing to your lord and master. He

64

said he would come and see one of my shows but I don't suppose he'll have the time.'

Beardsmore entered the conversation again, his tone almost insolent. 'This lady gave performances too. Mr Scott told us she was an amateur actress.'

Dr Holland paused to examine his carved-up patient. Then, with an expressionless face, he turned to Beardsmore. 'Well, if she's acting now, she's bloody good.'

In the station foyer it seemed that a party was going on. As Clement escorted Felling to the door, Shakila saw that a dozen or so officers were congregated around a stranger, a man in early middle age, casually dressed in jeans and a neatly collared polo shirt. His hand was being shaken and noisy jokes shared and the group grew larger as passing officers joined it. Shakila listened to snatches of the conversation.

'This week, it's been delivering bankruptcy notices. I deal with the women and she puts her feminine wiles to work on the men. Some people get aggressive but, if you stay polite, they usually come round. Touch wood, neither of us has been thumped yet.'

Shakila noticed that Caroline had appeared in the crowd in the foyer, looking rosy and wide awake again. 'Who is it?' she whispered after her colleague had shaken the man's hand and enquired after his health.

'He was Sergeant Warren, till he was shot in the knee and the foot on a drugs raid. That was two years ago. Now he's Colin Warren, private eye, and he pops in from time to time. We're useful to each other. We can sometimes slip information to him that he'd find it hard to come by and he can do things for us that aren't quite by the book.'

'What was the joke about the woman?'

Caroline grinned. 'I'm not sure about the facts, but rumour has it he's taken on a glamorous actress who's out of work.'

'Resting, they call it.'

'If you say so. Anyway, she tarts herself up, looking

different every day, which actresses should be good at, and does all the shadowing. It's certainly true he's got a woman assistant and he's definitely enjoying all the leg-pulling . . .'

Suddenly, several officers made for the stairs and the social gathering round Mr Warren melted away. Shakila saw that DCI Mitchell was approaching the outer door and she hurried out after the others.

After a few minutes, the anticipated call came through to Clement's cell phone. He and Shakila were to get some lunch and report to the DCI's office at one. They had been granted four extra DCs and some uniforms. Clement had no need to ask whether they were now on a murder investigation, though this provision of extra manpower was paltry.

The officers presented themselves early but had to wait until the whole team had assembled before Mitchell gave them any news. Clement spent the time looking the DCs over as they arrived. Two of them, David Guest and Peter Cranton, he knew by sight and a third, Elinor Curzon, he knew well as a fellow runner, though he had never worked with her.

The last to arrive was a stranger to Clement and failed his test immediately by ogling Caroline as he saw her in undamaged profile and wincing when she turned to greet him, revealing her scars.

Precisely at one o'clock, Mitchell collected their attention with a cool glance round the room. For the benefit of the newcomers he summarized the case so far and referred them to the details of that morning's post-mortem exam-ination, now in the file. 'For now it is enough to know that Dr Holland is satisfied that Lorraine Felling was deliber-ately suffocated. He was very careful to point out that the vomiting was caused by the asphyxia, not the other way round. The victim struggled and so would have taken less than the previously estimated five minutes to die. Even so, someone was prepared to take a big risk.

'There were forty-two guests present in the house besides the couple who live there. All of them moved about freely both before and after the crime was committed. A surgeon from the Infirmary kept everyone together after it was discovered.'

Smithson raised a hand. 'There were also two cooks from Peterson's based in the kitchen and three other people, youngsters employed fairly casually to serve and clear up. All of them had been used before though. Between them they were responsible for leaving the kitchen as they'd found it. I've put a list of names in the file. Apparently, Mrs Bates ordered lavishly. Her husband went in later, curtailed the order and put everything on sale or return.'

'They couldn't return food, surely?'

'Not if a pack of something had been opened, but they're an efficient company. They had a refrigerated van parked in the drive and took from it as required.'

'So, Barry Bates is a bit of a scrooge.'

Smithson shook his head. 'That wasn't what Peterson's thought – but he is a bank manager.'

'Having a lot of money doesn't mean you have to splash it around. People who're used to being rich understand that.' The latter remark came from a young PC, fresh from police college, and caused a ripple of amusement.

Mitchell turned to the noticeboard. 'This is Lorraine.' They all looked at two pictures, pinned side by side. In one an attractive blonde woman held a wine glass and laughed up at a companion who had been cut off between the eyes. In the other, the same woman, her face blotched, her eyes closed and her make-up smudged, lay on a stained pillow, covered by a stained lace spread.

There was silence for several seconds as they all looked, and were struck by the contrast. Then Mitchell ran quickly through the rest of the facts in the file. 'So,' he concluded, 'the assembled company included Lorraine's estranged partner who has consistently campaigned for the custody of their daughter, Donna. There was Donna herself, who, according to Mr Scott, was given to fantasizing, and the son Philip, now engaged to be married to a girl whose father employs him. This girl, Antonia Grant, attended the funeral but declined the social function because she had a crucial business appointment.'

Details were given, as far as they were known, of the burglary. Looking up, Mitchell caught a doubtful glance from his sergeant. 'Jennifer?'

'Are we a hundred per cent sure about this burglary?'

'You aren't?'

'Well, the story about the husband hiding things sounds a bit thin. What if Diane Bates hid the things herself?'

'You mean you think it's an insurance scam?'

'No, I mean I'm wondering if she's trying to blame an imaginary burglar for her sister's murder.'

'That she committed herself?' Mitchell sounded sceptical.

'Well, it's possible. It could be that Lorraine had inherited all the family money from Mr Smith.'

'Was there much? I suppose that's one of the first things we'll have to find out. Any other original thoughts? You might as well get them out of your systems. Shakila, you were being bashful about a pet theory this morning. If it was worth considering, let's discuss it now. It can't be more far-fetched than Jennifer's.'

Shakila bit her lip. 'It might, sir. I was wondering if Lorraine really was alive when her sister left her, as she thought, and if it was Dr – sorry, Mr Scott – who killed her when he went up, supposedly to help.' She glanced back at the two pictures of Lorraine. 'The few dead bodies I've seen have all looked as though the person who used to be there has – well, moved out.'

'Depends how long they've been dying,' one elderly PC offered.

'Or, in this case, how drink had affected the victim's normal appearance,' one of the borrowed DCs added.

Comments followed, everyone wanting to air a theory.

'How anxious was Nicholas Felling to have charge of his daughter? Was he trying to spite his ex once they broke up or did he consider her a bad mother?'

'Maybe he just wanted the child's company.'

'Or was sick of seeing money he handed over for maintenance being spent on drink.'

'We don't know that it was.'

When the team's offerings dried up, Mitchell issued his usual warning. 'Your action sheets tell you who to talk to. They don't tell you what to say. You let everyone talk about everything and you listen very hard. Don't interrupt unless they're way off the beam, and maybe not even then. Above all, don't ask leading questions to get support for your pet theory.' He sent a hard look in Shakila's direction.

Mitchell had elected to interview Donna himself and to take Caroline with him. As they went down the staircase to the foyer they heard guffaws and saw the desk sergeant sharing a joke with a constable from traffic division.

'It's obviously National Hilarity Day,' Mitchell remarked tartly but there was sufficient good humour in his tone for the PC to venture to share his joke. He had, he announced, booked the ghost of a former US President the previous afternoon. 'He said his name was Jack Kennedy. I told him it would pay him not to mess me about and I asked for his licence. There it was, "John F. Kennedy". Even the middle initial was right. I asked him who it was that really shot him. I could tell he was fed up with jokes about his name. I didn't make it worse with jokes about his van.'

'What was wrong with that?'

'Nearside said, "Say It With Flowers" and the off said, "Let Flowers Brighten Your Life". The whole shoot was covered with pink and blue flowers and gold leaves. I'm not surprised the poor beggar had his foot down. He'd be trying to drive too fast for anyone to make out the lettering or else trying not to be recognized while driving it.'

Mitchell left the officers in the foyer to their continued laughter and went to find some lunch. As he came into the canteen, he saw his superintendent about to leave it. Their eyes met over the trolley where 'patrons' were requested to place their used crockery and cutlery.

69

Carroll greeted him. 'What have we got then, Benny? You're wearing the expression of a schoolboy who has just read the noticeboard and seen that he's not only made the team but been chosen as captain too.'

Both men averted their eyes as the superintendent dutifully scraped the remains of his meal into the waste bin and stacked his plate on the trolley.

Mitchell listed his findings. 'We've got confirmation, though not in writing yet, that Lorraine Conroy was deliberately suffocated. We've got witness evidence that the victim was a dipso with three consecutive partners and two illegitimate children to show for them, one subsequently adopted. She was well liked, though, even popular. She died at her sister's house where they were holding a wake for their father.'

'She won't be well liked by her family then. She'll be causing them a second lot of funeral expenses before they've recovered from the first.'

'Too right, especially as the victim's sister was burgled during the church service.'

The superintendent gave Mitchell a stern look. 'You're making half of this up so that I'll allocate you some more men.'

Mitchell sniffed. 'It's the gospel truth. I'd hand in my resignation if I couldn't make up a more plausible story than that.'

Carroll went to resettle himself in the chair he had vacated minutes before. 'Get an extra coffee for me. You may as well eat while you're bringing me up to date.'

Resignedly, Mitchell joined the short queue, bringing his meal to Carroll's table as bidden. Between mouthfuls of battered fish and mushy peas, he provided a carefully pruned account of his activities during the morning and tried to sound grateful for the advice he was offered. Feeling he had made a good case for himself, he enquired hopefully about his serious chances of extra men.

The superintendent was apparently in jocular mood. 'It's going to depend on how many suspects you can dredge up.'

Mitchell smiled happily. 'One officer per suspect? Fine, I'll need forty-four of 'em.'

The DCI was not the only officer in the canteen who was thankful when, after a few minutes, Carroll mentioned an appointment with the ACC and departed. Now that he had paid his regular duty visit to 'eat with the men' and show his solidarity with them, their canteen would revert to being a superintendent-free refuge for the rest of the month.

Chapter Five

Mitchell returned with relief to working out how he could obtain, most humanely, the information he needed from a thirteen-year-old girl.

Interviewing children was fraught with hazards but was a very valuable exercise. They noticed things that adults either missed altogether or took for granted, and they told things that more circumspect adults would keep back.

On the other hand, the general public and the children's guardians hated the idea of them being interrogated, perhaps exploited. Mitchell was naturally and genuinely anxious not to cause any further suffering to a child who had just lost her mother in these particularly nasty circumstances. He would have preferred to have Jennifer with him. He was glad that her evidence would most likely nail their villain in court but he resented her absence from the present enquiry on this crucial first day. Still, Caroline would do very well instead.

Beardsmore, Mitchell noticed, had kept a low profile at the latest briefing after his temerity in arguing with his DCI that morning. He had gone away a few minutes ago, looking quite subdued, even though he had been trusted with the second interview of Neville Scott. The team had been surprised to see him given this responsibility. Beardsmore was not a detective and Scott was either a very well-qualified witness or, if some of his officers were to be believed, a villain. Beardsmore ought to have been wagging both tails.

Caroline was the only one with the temerity to question his decision, raising the matter as she drove them to Felling's apartment. Mitchell smiled. 'I took a gamble because I was sorry for him. I wanted to build up his confidence again because I think he's a good embryo cop.'

'Why were you sorry for him?'

'He was at the PM,' he reminded her. 'He had to rush out to throw up at the first incision. He came back after a bit, still groggy and just as things were becoming really messy. When Ray popped all the plastic bags of organs back in the body before sewing up he collapsed at my feet. I tried to cheer him up on the way back but he wouldn't have it. He said he bet at my first PM I just stood there and took it.'

'Did you?' She saw, to her amazement, that Mitchell was blushing.

'I stayed on my feet but all I remember is standing in a swirling blackness, and repeating one of my mother's Catholic prayers to myself. I bet you weren't fazed at all.'

Caroline laughed. 'Women aren't. They have the babies. They're expected to cope and clear up the mess when someone's ill or has an accident. It's in their nature.'

'I told Beardsmore that a much-respected detective presently at the station had had a similar experience to his. I'm afraid he thinks I meant you.'

Caroline grinned. 'If you said "respected detective" I expect he does. It'll be interesting to see whether Scott offers the same co-operation to a PC as he did to you.'

Having been apprised of their visit, Felling came out to meet them. He was not happy. 'Is it really necessary to put Donna through this?' he demanded without greeting them.

Mitchell answered him evenly. 'I attended the post-mortem examination on your partner earlier today. We are now certain that Lorraine was suffocated deliberately, so, yes, it is. Children are keenly observant and we need her help. Whether she needs to know at this stage that she is helping with a murder enquiry is for you to decide.'

Felling capitulated at once and took them upstairs. He was casually dressed but his jeans and T-shirt were black. Donna wore a red mini-skirt and a red, white and blue rugby shirt with a black armband. Mitchell wondered whether the latter was worn in mockery of her father or in solidarity with him.

Since breakfast time, the effects of the sedative had worn off and Donna now looked bright-eyed and alert though solemn. She sat cross-legged on the end of her father's bed. Felling offered the only armchair to Caroline and a dining chair to Mitchell and remained standing himself.

Donna glanced at Caroline and then stared. 'What happened to your face?'

Donna had passed Caroline's test. A direct question was one of the reactions to her disfigurement that she permitted. Now, she settled herself into the armchair. 'It was cut when someone took a glass bottle to me.'

'It makes it worse that you're so good-looking from the other side.' Mitchell knew exactly what the girl meant.

'Does it?'

'I think so. Does your husband mind that it got spoilt?'

Caroline silenced the father with a glance and administered her own rebuke. 'I know you're only thirteen, Donna, but that's quite old enough to know your last question is off limits.'

'I'm sorry. I thought it was better to say what I thought than to leave you wondering.'

Caroline smiled. 'I'm glad you have that attitude. It's the one we want to take with you about your mother and all the things that happened yesterday.'

'You think somebody did it to her, don't you?'

Mitchell glanced at Felling, who went to sit beside his daughter on the bed. He reached for her hand but she drew it back. 'You're right,' he told her. 'Dr Holland, our pathologist, has found out that someone killed your mother.'

There was silence for several seconds until Donna broke it. 'Was it the burglar?'

This cool reaction shocked the girl's father more than the two officers. Caroline answered her. 'We have some police doctors who are pretty much on the ball. They looked at your mum very carefully this morning and they can prove that she was killed. They can't tell us who did it though. We have to find that out by talking to people who were there.'

The girl's brow wrinkled. 'But, if they did it, they'll tell lies – and lots of people tell lies anyway. People always do.'

'Do you know, you're the third young person, all in very different circumstances, to say exactly the same thing to us. It's good to know that the young folk understand our problems.'

Mitchell took charge again. 'It helps if even some people are as truthful as they can manage. Can you describe to us all you can remember about what happened at your aunt's house yesterday? Tell us about what you were thinking as well as what you saw.'

They watched as Donna projected herself back to the reception and mentally entered the house in Elm Road. Her eyes narrowed. 'What I thought at first was that Auntie Di was being either mean and spiteful or else just stupid for getting in all that wine and stuff. It was as if she was willing Mum to make a fool of herself. Then I thought that at least there were plenty of relations around so it wouldn't be me having to cope with Mum when she got drunk.' Tears rolled down Felling's cheeks but he remained silent.

Donna uncrossed her feet and hung her legs over the side of the bed as she considered what else to tell. 'When Mum started dancing, I wanted to laugh. Everyone pretended to be disgusted but most of them were cheering her on inside. To please Auntie Di, they were all saying she should know better and be more respectful to Grandad. I think he'd have wet himself laughing if he could have seen them all. I was wondering whether to dance with her, but then Mr Denby came in.'

'Mr Denby?'

'Grandad's mate. He's really old and uses a stick. I got up to give him my armchair. It was the one nearest the door so he wouldn't have to walk far. He said thank you but he looked sad and I wished I'd just got up and wandered off without saying anything. He looked like a guy

75

that somebody had made for a bonfire. I don't mean he was scruffy,' she added, quickly, 'but he looked as if his clothes were holding his body together. His face looks young, though. It's got thin pink skin like a baby's. People like him think men should always stand up for ladies. I tried to think of something else to say and I told him Grandad had been teaching me to play chess. He cheered up all right then. Said I wouldn't have to miss him for that because he'd teach me instead.' The two officers exchanged glances. In some ways, it seemed, Lorraine Conroy had made a very good job indeed of raising this daughter.

'Then Mum turned the music up really loud and I thought he'd be one of the crossest but he laughed and said that Grandad would be giving her his blessing. I like him but I wished he hadn't got me trapped. He started telling me stories about the old days but I'd heard them all before.'

'Did someone rescue you?'

Donna sniffed. 'Only the vicar. He looked different from before. In church he'd had long black and white clothes and a coloured silk scarf thing and looked special. At Auntie Di's he was all in black except for his dog collar and he looked ordinary and nearly as old as Mr Denby. I knew he was going to say how was I getting on at school and he did.'

'I suppose,' Mitchell suggested, 'that it's the one thing that older people can expect any boy or girl to know about. A lot of older people don't understand football or pop music or computers but at least they know what it feels like to go to school. Did you find something to tell him about yours?'

Donna shook her head. 'No, I asked him what his hobbies were and what made him want to be a vicar.' Mitchell laughed out loud and even Felling smiled.

'What did you do next?'

'I went to the dining room to look at the lily-of-the-valley egg.'

Mitchell's expression sharpened. 'The Fabergé one?'

The girl shrugged. 'She said so. Mum said it was a fake. It's lovely, anyway. It's got lily flowers made of tiny pearls and they're fastened in silver wire that's twisted in a pattern all over a pink egg. I like looking at it so much it almost makes up for having to go and see Auntie Di.' Mitchell made a note in his book. Was Lorraine speaking with any knowledge of Fabergé artefacts, or merely goading her sister? For now, he would not interrupt the flow of the girl's evidence.

'So,' Caroline asked carefully, 'did looking at it cheer you up yesterday?'

Donna turned from Mitchell back to her and shook her head. 'No, it wasn't there. I hoped she hadn't sold it to pay for her fancy party. If she has I'll never go again. Anyway, Micky was in there – that's the cat – so I played with him for a bit.' Mitchell and Caroline exchanged glances. Did the Bateses have money troubles?

Donna seemed to have finished all she wanted to say. She sat hugging her knees and staring vacantly ahead. Before Felling could intervene, Mitchell said, 'Thank you for that very clear account. Now we have just a few quick questions that only need short answers. What perfume did your mother use? I didn't ask your father. We men never notice these things.'

Donna nodded in agreement. 'It was usually Chanel No. 5 when she could afford it or she got some for a present. She had a friend who bought it for her.' This time the two detectives managed not to look at each other. If possible, they would ask for the friend's name when Donna was being chaperoned by someone other than her father.

'That isn't the one she was wearing yesterday.'

The girl's expression brightened. 'No, that was Californian Poppy. I spent all the money from my newspaper round on it to cheer her up when Grandad died. She specially put it on for the funeral.'

Mitchell was liking Lorraine increasingly. 'Have you got that, Caroline? It's important.'

Donna was flattered. 'I've got the rest of the bottle if you need it.'

'When you have the chance to go home and get it, that will be very useful.'

'Her home's with me now!'

Both officers blinked at Felling's sharp tone. 'Of course. You've both been very patient and we've almost finished. Can you think very carefully, Donna, about the time between when your mother was taken upstairs and when Mr Scott came down to tell everyone she'd died?' For the first time, the girl's composure slipped and she bit her lip. Felling glared a warning at the two officers. 'Have you any definite memory of who went upstairs? Only say if you're quite sure.'

'I was sitting on the stairs after Philip and Dad came down, so I am sure. Auntie Di went up to do her face again. She went up with a shiny nose and lipstick on her teeth and came back all prim and powdery again.'

Caroline hid a smile. 'Anyone else?

Donna wrinkled her nose. 'That fat doctor that Mum was friendly with went up to the loo. He was up there for ages. P'raps he was making himself beautiful as well. Oh, and my brother sneaked up for a kiss and a cuddle with Snooty Lady . . .'

Felling shook his head. 'I don't think so, Donna. Toni had to go to work straight after the service. She didn't come to Auntie Di's.'

Donna's grief was temporarily forgotten and her face lit up. 'You mean he was snogging somebody else? Bags I be the one to tell her.' She turned back to Caroline as Mitchell made a quick observation in his notebook. 'I also saw a man who was a stranger. He said "Excuse me" when I moved for him, which is more than Philip did. He also . . .' She paused to consider the extent of Caroline's credulity. 'He had a front gold tooth and one of those thick black plastic bags under his arm. If he'd put the swag in it, he could have got it out by dropping it from a bedroom window to his accomplice on the terrace.'

Mitchell's expression remained deadpan. 'Can you remember anything else about this man?'

But Donna had been reprimanded by a glance from her father and merely shook her head. The sparkle of mischief had gone when she said solemnly, 'I'm quite sure my father didn't go up.'

'We've heard,' Caroline put in, 'that your mother had taken a job. What was it?'

Donna pouted. 'She wouldn't tell me. She said the less anyone knew about it the better for all concerned.' This denial of her mother's confidence had obviously rankled.

Mitchell deliberately waited until they had risen to go and both Fellings were off their guard before asking their last question. 'When your aunt came into the dining room at some point yesterday, she noticed you were moving chair cushions and covers, looking for something you'd lost. Could you tell us what it was?'

Donna's face flamed and then paled. Mitchell held her gaze until she muttered, 'I can't remember,' and transferred it to her father in mute appeal.

Felling's face was white with fury. 'It doesn't matter, Donna. It's not important.' He left the room with the two officers, closing the door behind them all. In an angry whisper he rounded on them. 'If my daughter doesn't get over this, I shall hold you responsible. If you must know, she'd lost her diary. Can you remember what you put in yours when you were thirteen? Who'd kissed you behind the bike sheds? What happened on a date – or, more likely, what you wish had happened? Maybe which teacher you had a crush on? I found it and gave it back to her and she was on pins until I assured her I hadn't opened it. Satisfied?'

He left them abruptly, returned to his room and closed the door with a resounding slam.

The *Cloughton Clarion* had made what it could out of the meagre information that had been released. It was a weekly publication, going to press late on Tuesday night, so that holding back for more might mean that the matter would be resolved before readers had been informed of the death and word of mouth would have made the *Clarion*'s report redundant. Though facts were scanty, the leader writer had risen to the challenge.

Philip Conroy, calling on Felling, had brought Wednesday's copy, hot from the press. Felling read through the leading article carefully.

DOUBLE TRAGEDY AT SMITH CLAYTON FUNERAL
The home of Mr Barry and Mrs Diane Bates was the scene of a double tragedy yesterday evening. The £450,000 house was the setting for the reception of guests who had attended the funeral of local businessman, Mr Edgar James Smith, the recently retired Chairman of Smith Clayton engineering of Keighley Road, Cloughton. As the invited guests relaxed after their traumatic day and reminisced about the life and achievements of Mr Smith, his elder daughter Lorraine collapsed and had to be helped to bed.

'We knew she was devastated by our father's death,' Mrs Bates told our reporter, 'but we didn't realize she was ill.' Some time later, Mrs Lorraine Conroy was found to have died in her sleep. 'We can't arrange a funeral service for Lorraine,' said Mrs Bates today. 'The death was so sudden that there will have to be an inquest.'

Mrs Conroy's son Philip, who was present at the reception, is engaged to be married. 'We shall put off the arrangements for our wedding indefinitely,' he said today, 'out of respect for my mother.' His fiancée is Miss Antonia Grant, only child of Victor Grant whose textile and clothing company of the same name has signed contracts for a sum in excess of £3 million with three national chain stores this year.

Mr Conroy also works for Victor Grant, as a sales manager.

A source close to the family revealed that Mrs Lorraine Conroy was chief beneficiary in Mr Smith's

80

will. His personal estate is valued at approximately £500,000.

Felling let out a low whistle as he came to the last sentence. 'I'd no idea Edgar was worth so much.'

Philip shook his head. 'Nor me. I wonder who Mum's left it all to.'

Felling folded the paper neatly and put it on the table. 'Knowing Lorraine, I shouldn't think she's left it to anyone. Can you see her having made a will?'

'So, what will happen?'

Felling looked irritated. 'I teach English, not law. It should be easy enough to find out. On second thoughts, perhaps there is a will. If Edgar knew that Lorraine was going to be so wealthy, he may well have twisted her arm to be sensible about it. Anyway, money's hardly the most important question just now.'

'I know someone who wouldn't agree.'

'That's your only aunt you're maligning.'

'She's the only aunt I know about anyway, but actually I was thinking of Uncle Barry. He'll know what's going to happen to it all. He might not say much but he's nobody's fool.'

'Perhaps he keeps quiet so that Diane can't misquote him.'

'That's no protection. I've said nothing to her or to any reporter, but here I am in the *Clarion*, postponing my marriage when I haven't persuaded Toni to fix a date for it yet.'

'Perhaps your aunt decided to invent some finer feelings for you.'

'Thanks a lot. Do you realize that this rag gives my future father-in-law no fewer than four mentions on the front page alone?'

Felling wondered why this seemed to annoy Philip. To humour him, he looked back at the *Clarion* and scanned the long narrow column that dealt with the senior citizens' orchestra's concert that was to take place on the following Saturday. 'I'd forgotten he played in the oldies' band.'

'He's quite good on the trumpet,' Philip allowed grudgingly. 'I've heard him a couple of times at carol concerts at St Barnabas'.'

'They haven't put him in the headline, though. He only gets a mention in the third paragraph. Where else is he?'

Philip pointed to an article headed 'Local Company Sports Includes County Record.' 'Victor didn't break it himself, of course. It was a young lad who started in the packing department this summer. Somebody Stepney, a nice kid but a bit simple. Cracking runner, though. Vic would have done well to have kept his mouth shut about his athletic prowess at school. He was scraping the barrel a bit. His times would have been better not mentioned.'

Felling was still searching the front page. 'That's only three times – oh, you mean the usual advertisement for the company? That's always there. I never look at it.'

Philip laughed. 'I'll tell him. Maybe we can cut down on the advertising budget.'

Pleading pressure of work, he left, but Felling did not believe he had offended him.

Barry Bates sighed as he sank into a leather armchair, taking for granted rather than enjoying its blissful comfort. He would, with hindsight, still have married Diane, but he had hoped that by now he would have learned how to please her. The trouble was, she never knew quite what she wanted. Having for many years adamantly refused to spoil her figure and her lifestyle by having children, she now seemed, by some freakish reasoning, to consider it his fault that they had not produced just one perfect example.

He too would have liked a child, but their idea of perfection in the species didn't chime. Diane wanted a daughter to dress up and to share her trivial interests. He would have liked a son, so that he could come home to discuss something more important than interior decoration, or whether a particular garment made Diane look fat.

She looked fat in everything because she was fat – and he wouldn't care about that if she didn't.

Now she had her eye on Donna. It was amazing that Lorraine's girl fitted the bill for Diane. The child must have inherited some genes from a socially acceptable father – though sleeping with Lorraine didn't, in Barry's book, say much for his social acceptability. Donna! What a stupid name! What was wrong with the good, old-fashioned ones? Nevertheless, she was an interesting character, certainly tough. She'd dealt with her mother in a way she should never have had to. Diane said she was biddable, but he couldn't imagine his niece doing anything she didn't approve or see the point of. Nothing wrong with that, of course. In fact, she was a thoroughly nice girl, but he didn't want to take her on. Before long, Diane would begin to find her intractable. The child had a bigger heart and more serious ambitions than her aunt, not to mention the trouble it would stir up with Nick.

Maybe his greatest, and so far unacknowledged, objection to the scheme was that Diane had at no point consulted him when making her plans. She'd seen only as far as companionship for herself and approval from her friends for doing her duty by her family.

Barry was relieved to have his uncomfortable meditations interrupted by Diane's appearance in the drawing-room doorway. She ambled over to the sofa that matched his chair and sank down on to it. Air was expelled from its cushions producing the sort of unseemly noise that made Donna giggle. 'Make the drinks strong, Barry,' she instructed him, dropping their copy of the *Cloughton Clarion* on the seat beside her and wiping her perspiring face with one of her myriad lace-edged handkerchiefs.

He rose to pour his own whisky with a dash of soda, which he sipped as he prepared the complicated cocktail Diane currently favoured. 'What's driven you to strong drink?'

Diane indicated the bottom half of the *Clarion*'s front page. 'They've soon made us the talk of the town. Shall I read it to you?'

He nodded, knowing that nothing would stop her, but presumed to interrupt from time to time. 'Is this place really worth nearly half a million now?'

'I should hope so!' She read on, pausing to ask, 'How many people, reading that, will guess what made Lorraine collapse?'

'Same number as knew her drinking habits before, so no harm done. Did you really say all that stuff about her to that reporter?'

'What did you expect me to say? That, at our father's funeral, she was legless and dancing?'

'On her hands, you mean? That would have been clever, even for Lorraine.'

'When will the inquest be?'

Barry shrugged and handed his wife her well-shaken brew. 'Pretty soon, but the police will just ask for an adjournment pending enquiries.'

Diane continued her reading with commentary. 'It's good of Philip to put his plans on hold, but I hope he gets on with things fairly quickly. I know they're engaged now, but his wasn't Toni's only offer.'

Barry finished his drink but decided to put off 'refreshing' it until Diane was distracted. 'I didn't realize Victor was doing so well. Will Philip be able to cope with such a big concern when the time comes?'

Diane finished the article without answering. She was too proud to comment on the unfairness of the huge bequest to her sister. Barry didn't dare.

The Jacksons too were enjoying an end-of-the-day drink. Cavill let his eyes travel idly down the front page of the *Clarion* since his wife, her eyes shut as she let the day's concerns drift away, seemed disinclined for conversation. When she sat up and reached for her glass, he asked, indicating the relevant article, 'How much of that have they invented and how much is true?'

Caroline smiled. 'Answering that is our job for tomorrow.'

'If I'd realized how much money there was in the family, I'd have charged them more. The organ fund could do with it, not to mention the old folks' band.'

'Come off it! Your orchestra's far from broke, thanks to Mr Grant. Anyway, mightn't there be a small bequest to that? Edgar put in his twopennyworth when he was alive so . . .'

Cavill nodded. 'Yes, possibly. I wonder if St Barnabas' will be chosen for the indefinitely postponed nuptials.'

'They're more likely to pick a swish hotel for the ceremony.' She grinned. 'Maybe they'll invite the senior cits to play there.' She picked up the paper and glanced through the short paragraphs again. 'Who do you think the source close to the family is?'

'I'd guess old Walter Denby.'

'We've been told by several people that he was pretty drunk. Can we trust his figures?'

'Don't underestimate Walter. Drunk or sober, he's nobody's fool.'

Walter Denby washed down more paracetamol with strong tea as he reread the *Clarion* account with horror at his own small contribution in particular. How much liquor had he put away last night? He had no recollection whatsoever of speaking to any reporter. Perhaps it hadn't been him. There were sources closer to the family than himself, but they should have had no knowledge of any financial details. So – he was still to blame. Whoever else it was who might have shared this private family matter with the whole of Cloughton, that person must have got the information from himself. He made a silent apology to Edgar and hoped a public one would not be demanded by Diane.

Antonia Grant was reasonably pleased with the results of what she had fed to the reporter from the *Clarion*. She thanked a kindly providence that had sent him to her late

85

on Tuesday night, when hovering round the Bateses' house had earned him only a thorough rousting from the police. She was lucky too that it was young Chris the paper had sent. He owed her a few favours and here was one of them paid back. He had put in the supposed quotation from Philip word for word as she had dictated it. That should give her some thinking time.

Did she really want to marry Philip? He was quite good-looking, probably the best of her options in that department. He was certainly not the next Mr Gates. He did have enough nous, though, to keep the firm running sufficiently smoothly to continue filling their bank accounts. She couldn't put her finger on why she was becoming so dissatisfied with him.

Lorraine had been an increasing problem, of course. The tabloids would have had a field day with the antics she would have got up to at their wedding. Perhaps she'd never been sure and worries about his mother had distracted her from doubts about Philip himself. He didn't excite her. He never surprised her.

She remembered first meeting him at a party with his family – or, at least, some of them. She smiled as she relived the occasion in her head. It had been a Victor Grant Christmas party and she hadn't wanted to go. Her father had insisted and she had resigned herself to an evening of utter boredom. Lorraine had behaved in her usual fashion and had provided – with her blowsy appearance, honest local accent and cheerful refusal to conform – just the sort of diversion the evening needed to make it entertaining. Philip had been twenty-one then. Dad had promoted him to please her when it became obvious that she'd taken a shine to him. She didn't think he would have been picked out otherwise – plenty of intelligence but not enough push.

As she'd got to know him, he'd shown some of Lorraine's refreshing characteristics but with the rough edges smoothed away. Now, she could see that what she had thought to be interesting quirks in Philip were just the result of their widely diverging backgrounds and upbringing. Lorraine had been a true eccentric. Philip had seemed to be one only because his expectations, attitudes and behaviour were such as she hadn't come up against before. He'd struggled – and succeeded – to fit in with the Grants' ways and had abandoned that part of him which had appealed to her. Well, she'd have to see what would happen now.

Glenda Grant was also about to read the by-now notorious article. She found the *Clarion* on the mat as she came into the house and carried it into the sitting room where Victor was reading the mail that had accumulated during his absence. She indicated the short double column. 'We've made the bottom of the front page with our double death. In spite of not being there, you've managed to get yourself mentioned twice.'

'I hope it's to my advantage. What does it say?'

'That your firm – yours, notice, not ours – has signed contracts for a sum in excess of three million. Is that right?'

'It's in the right area but that's turnover, not profit.'

'Still enough to pay for whatever it took to get her off your back. Pick more carefully in future, Vic.'

Leaving him spluttering she quietly left the room, taking the *Clarion* with her.

Virginia Mitchell had timed her meal to be ready at the exact hour that her husband had promised to be home. Well, he'd at least half promised, which was as much as he could offer them when he was in the middle of a case. The children had already left for school when he had eventually come in that morning and they were beginning to realize now that they would have to go to bed without seeing him tonight.

She put the *Clarion* back in the magazine rack, having glanced over the first page, and marched into the dining room, determinedly cheerful. 'Never mind. The sausages will taste just as good without Daddy here and you'll all be able to have an extra one.'

Caitlin's mournful expression did not change. 'No, they won't. He makes us laugh so we don't think about them being burnt.'

If ever a meal took place when it was supposed to, Virginia thought crossly, her food might taste as it was supposed to. She tried another distraction. 'Daddy's work is very important. It keeps us – and everyone else in Cloughton – safer.'

Sinead nodded sagely. 'He catches all the bad men.'

Declan, for once in argumentative mood, challenged her. 'No, he doesn't. He only catches some of them.'

Caitlin, as always, backed him up. 'Yes – or he sends Auntie Jennifer to get them if they're bad ladies.'

Michael, who usually attended solemnly to family discussions, absorbing information and opinions but keeping his own counsel, felt this was the occasion for a rare question. 'Mummy, when do the bad people get bad? Are they born bad babies?'

Offering her younger son no thanks for this conversation stopper, Virginia began dishing out overdone sausages. 'Ask your father,' she told him, remembering too late that it was Benny's absence that they had all been grumbling about.

At six that evening, as he began his debriefing, Mitchell was finding it difficult to stay awake. He would, he decided, just collect in his team's reports and then have a long night's sleep before reviewing his options. If he let the team go now, he could demand a hundred and twenty per cent attention and effort the next day.

He grinned round blearily at his shift. 'The house-to-house enquirers can have first go. They usually have to wait till the end when we've all stopped listening.' The men grinned back but none of them had anything very helpful to report. There had been a great willingness to co-operate but, since there was a big funeral happening, the inhabitants of Elm Road had expected to see strangers about and had politely refrained from staring at them. The more elderly neighbours had followed their generation's custom, showing their respect for the deceased by drawing their curtains, and so had seen nothing at all.

Mitchell allowed Caroline to give an account of Donna's evidence, which was received with a good deal of scepticism by most of the officers.

'Did she say how long she was sitting on the stairs?' someone asked.

Caroline shook her head. 'Since she warned us – and Scott did – that she was going to tell us a pack of lies, it may not really matter.'

Mitchell could not agree. 'We need to take it all with a good pinch of salt, but that doesn't mean that nothing she says is true.'

'She said Diane Bates went upstairs before the occasion when she needed the trays?' As Caroline nodded confirmation, they all turned to Beardsmore. 'Doesn't that support Sergeant Taylor's theory that she killed her sister and then removed her own possessions as a blind?'

Mitchell reconsidered the idea. 'It's possible, but we shouldn't get fanciful. It's more likely that there was an intruder.'

Jennifer was loath to relinquish her more interesting idea in favour of the mundane one. 'It could be an insurance scam as someone suggested before, that, unfortunately for the Bateses, coincided with the murder of Lorraine by someone else.'

'Donna suggested they weren't as well off as they'd like people to think.'

'But we can't believe her.'

'I think we can probably believe that.' They waited for Caroline to explain herself. 'I think we can trust the things she only implied more than the things she actually said.'

'I don't follow, Caro.'

'Well, she makes up stories but I don't think she's sophisticated enough to throw out a casual remark, like the one about Diane's jewelled egg paying for all the goodies, and leave us to draw our own conclusions.'

'So, it slipped out and might very well be true?'

Caroline nodded. 'Yes, I think the little aside about selling the egg was quite involuntary.'

'Or was it her idea of a joke?'

'Maybe. What about this job of Lorraine's? Temping could mean anything. Has she got involved in something illegal and had her mouth shut for her?'

'Drugs, you mean?'

'Possibly.'

Mitchell felt they were being sidetracked. He turned to one of the borrowed DCs. 'Elinor, you'd better get on to the temping agencies and see if you can find out where Lorraine has been employed. Meanwhile, I think we should keep looking at Felling. He was in an invidious position. He wanted Donna to be with him. He obviously wanted to rescue her from the awful responsibility of a parent the worse for drink – the constant dread of it as well as the horror of it actually happening. While he must have reproved himself for not protecting Donna, he realized that Lorraine might disintegrate totally if she didn't have the child as her reason for holding herself together at least to some extent.'

He glanced up and caught Beardsmore's eye, glad to see the lad looked perky and pleased with himself again. Mitchell invited him to tell them what he had learned from Neville Scott.

'I didn't see him, sir. He flew out to Saudi this afternoon to operate on some rich Arab.'

Mitchell was dismayed and angry. 'He must know he's totally out of order. He talked about having to operate this morning. Surely, if this was a genuine trip in the course of his work, he'd have mentioned it.'

Beardsmore was unfazed. 'I thought the same as you, sir, that he'd left the country to avoid us, but he'd have a lot to lose. He's got a good post here.'

'Rich Arabs'd pay him more,' Jennifer muttered darkly.

'I chatted to his theatre nurse,' Beardsmore continued.

'She's known for a fortnight that he was going. She says he'll be back on Friday.'

Mitchell was reassured to some extent by this information. Looking round at his officers and considering his options, he noticed that Shakila seemed very pleased with herself. 'So what did you do this afternoon?' he asked her.

'Well, I was going to join the house-to-house officers because I'd got to the end of my action sheet. Then I suddenly remembered a neighbour telling my brother, a month or so ago, about a friend who'd been to a funeral. Apparently the husband of the deceased had come back to his house and found it had been broken into. I thought I'd just spend a few minutes on the computer to see if there were any more incidents to match up with the one at Elm Road.'

'And I suppose from that smug look on your face that you were right.'

Shakila nodded happily and handed over the report she had had time to type out whilst her colleagues were out. 'There doesn't seem to be any common factor for victims – all income brackets and a wide variety of districts in Cloughton and round about it. Sometimes just one thing was taken, sometimes quite a lot, but it was always money or things that are easy to carry and valuable.'

Mitchell beamed at her. 'Well done, though I hestitate to thank you. Following it up will need another army of officers that we haven't got. We'll have to do it, though.'

'I worked out,' Shakila finished triumphantly, 'that every incident, and there were eleven of them, involved one of three funeral directors.'

'Well, seeing how you're managing all on your own, I'll leave it to you. Check out all three thoroughly and be back in five minutes.'

Once she had ascertained that the teasing was good-natured, Shakila laughed and settled back to listen further. Mitchell read extracts from an interim forensic report before tucking it into the file. 'It'll be virtually impossible to match up prints all over the house with yesterday's guests, the family and assorted casual visitors. There are less in the spare bedroom though. We may be able to eliminate the family there and see what we're left with. There is a thumbprint on the bedhead where someone might have supported himself as he leaned over Lorraine. Forensic are busy with the thumbs of the guests.

'I expect you've all seen the front page of the *Clarion*. It's not evidence but it's a timely reminder of how much money is involved in the deaths of some members of this family. We know what was in Edgar's will but we still aren't sure whether Lorraine made one or which solicitor she used if she did. We need to find out as much as possible about the Bateses' finances too. Sleep well. You'll all be busy in the morning.'

Mitchell could hardly believe how much work he and his team had crammed into one long Wednesday.

Later that same Wednesday night, after the Victor Grant factory closed down for the day, Philip Conroy sat on in his office, determined to bring his paperwork up to date. He enjoyed playing with figures. His employer well understood his immediate family situation and there was no pressure on him to make atonement for his absence. It was Philip, not Victor Grant, who became irritated if the plans for his department were not carried out according to the strict timetable he had set himself.

He could make things work here. His family life, in contrast, had always been in complete chaos and there had been very little he could do about it. It soothed him to shut out the muddle, to take refuge in his office with a spreadsheet on his computer screen that responded obediently when he pressed the right keys.

He was annoyed when he heard a tap on the door until he saw that his visitor was Victor Grant himself. His future father-in-law smiled uncertainly. 'Saw the light on. Just checking it wasn't intruders. I thought you and Toni were out on the town tonight.'

Reluctantly Philip saved his document, cleared his

screen and turned in his swivel chair. 'I'm not in the mood and, anyway, she won't go. She won't appear in public until her face is back to normal. Do you think she should go on riding that animal? He certainly lives up to his name.'

'It would take a braver man than I am to separate Toni and Bonkers. What surprises me is her admission that he threw her. I know he's done it before and she's always invented a cover story.'

'Well, it wasn't on this time. No one's going to believe she rolled in a patch of blackberry bushes for fun so she's had to come clean.'

Grant perched on the corner of Philip's desk. 'Actually, it could have been a very nasty accident. There was a chunk of barbed wire tangled in with the briars that made a small but nasty wound, though the rest is just superficial. The cut was only just below her eye. She could have blinded herself. Anyway, luckily, she didn't. Seen this?'

Grant flung his copy of the *Clarion* on to Philip's desk. Both men registered with distaste the picture of Lorraine looking like a performer in a nightclub cabaret.

Philip skimmed through the article again. 'I see Auntie Di's in inventive mode. I'm sure they paid just under two hundred grand for the house. It's worth a bit more now, of course, even with recessions and a depressed market – and I certainly wouldn't grumble if she gave it to me. I wonder where they got all this stuff about the will. Auntie Di wouldn't have blabbed that.'

Grant sniffed. 'It's funny what reporters think are important. There's more about what people are worth than about Edgar's life and achievements, or Lorraine's. Look, Philip, I know this is a bad time for you, but I need you to look at the Cat Walk contract if you could.'

'Tonight?'

'I'm sorry, forget it. I shouldn't have asked. I was going to do it myself when I thought you and Toni were wining and dining.'

Philip reached for the relevant file, assuring Grant, with perfect sincerity, that he would be positively glad to spend the rest of the evening over a tough contract and a couple of beers.

Clement too had stayed at his desk after the debriefing, doing his paperwork. His, however, was done of necessity and finished very thankfully. Now he was packing his working clothes into his rucksack and putting on the gear in which he had run to work that morning.

Elinor's nose always wrinkled on the days they ran part of the way home together and he laughed at the fastidiousness that made her carry spare running gear as well as her working clothes, so that she could go home in a fresh vest and shorts under her tracksuit. She was unimpressed by Clement's argument that, as soon as she began working hard, the clean clothes too would smell foul.

He reached home restored and exhilarated and feeling less tired than when he had set off. He drank a pint of water, showered and pulled on his dressing gown. Then he filled in his running diary and regretfully faced the fact that the Great North Run would be one competitor short again this year. It was his favourite event and this was the second year on the trot that work had prevented his taking part. Still, there was no way he would be spared from the case for a pleasure trip to Newcastle.

Chapter Six

On Thursday morning, Shakila left Pugh's, Cloughton's most prestigious funeral director, depressed by both the sanctimonious luxury of its furnishings and the driving rain through which she had had to dash to and from her car. She was not sure how useful the information she had gleaned was going to be.

Mr Pugh himself had been available and had pronounced himself willing to give all assistance that the police might require. He had been taken aback, though, when Shakila had asked him to describe the whole organization of his firm in detail.

He had resorted to heavy humour. 'Buried someone alive, have we? Made a batch of coffins out of oak that fell off the back of a lorry? Or maybe we're guilty of bad taste. Perhaps one of the bearers blew his nose on too brightly coloured a handkerchief.'

Shakila waited patiently until Mr Pugh's seam of facetiousness was exhausted. Then she repeated her request for each process to be explained. Mr Pugh remained cooperative and allowed her to speak briefly with all employees on the premises. Now she wondered gloomily how long the paperwork on this morning's findings was going to take her.

She realized, however, as she entered the equally church-like foyer of Merrill & Taylor, that she would be able to ask more specific questions here. Now she had a general idea of the whole business and more details than she was comfortable with of the various services a funeral director offered. She asked Mr Taylor for a list of the company's suppliers and the names of all his employees who would have reason to know the addresses of clients and details of their requirements, particularly the exact times of the various ceremonies.

Shakila was finished here in half the time she had taken at Pugh's and had her list of questions all ready to use on Westwood & Smith. When she'd been there, she'd deserve a cup of coffee in the canteen. She felt more than a little resentful, on arriving there, to find Superintendent Carroll berating a group of constables who had similarly rewarded themselves.

She dodged out quickly into the corridor and obtained a polystyrene cupful of an inferior brew from the machine in the alcove. Against all regulations, she carried it off and drank it as she sat at a computer terminal. Hardly tasting the bitter brew, she tapped keys happily, pausing now and then to add to her scribbled notes. Pugh's and Merrill's did embalming but Westwood's did not. Merrill's and Pugh's made coffins on part of their premises from wood sent in by a national supplier whilst Westwood's bought ready-made coffins from a local joiner. Merrill's and Westwood's employed the same cleaning woman, the former using her after closing in the evening and the latter before opening. Pugh's was valeted by a team from the office cleaning service in town.

Bingo! Shakila drained her beaker and a happy smile transformed her dark features. All three firms had a contract with Flowers in Truscott Street to supply floral decorations and tributes for clients who had not opted to make their own arrangements.

Jennifer made her usual quick check through the file before beginning on her scheduled tasks for the morning. Elinor's account of her fruitless series of enquiries at Cloughton's two temping agencies made depressing reading. Both of them denied finding employment for any Lorraine, whether she be Conroy or Felling.

She was no more enthusiastic about her own forthcoming visit to Philip Conroy, even though she was intrigued by the young man. So many of the people she had questioned had offered an opinion of him. Felling had found him difficult, yet seemed to like him. Diane, according to Clement, had been genuinely delighted when he had appeared at the hotel the previous morning. That could have been because he was good at managing his sister, or because he was engaged to and bringing into the family a young woman of the type Diane would wish to claim as a friend and relative: wealthy, stylish, a power in the land. There had been no ill-natured gibes about her nephew himself, nor about his illegitimacy.

Jennifer found that his address was an irritating, mock Georgian compound of 'luxury apartments'. Wherever, she wondered, could you find the non-luxury variety with which their comforts were to be contrasted? Its background of uncompromising Victorian terraces, rising up the hillside behind, gave the block a slightly ridiculous air. Perhaps the architect had become aware of this defect. It could have been the reason why, in two places, he had interrupted the flat line of windows with huge, pillastered, pseudo-Victorian bays. His ruse had not worked.

One of the bays seemed to belong to her quarry who proved to be rather more physically attractive than his home. He was dark and well groomed, not startlingly handsome but attractive with good teeth and an intelligent expression. 'You've got a hell of a job!' he informed Jennifer. 'Probably a good half of the forty-odd people at the Bateses' house went upstairs while my mother was in the spare room – for the loo, to titivate, to satisfy their curiosity or to get away from the loud music.

'And, if you give up on opportunity and try motive, you're no better off. My mother spent almost all her life racketing around in a perpetual financial crisis but she never made demands or sponged on anyone. Almost everyone disapproved of her but hardly anyone disliked her. Those who found her irritating could keep out of her way. No one wanted her to die.'

'You're very dispassionate.' Jennifer settled herself comfortably in the armchair she had been allocated.

'I'm a dispassionate sort of man. And, although I loved my mother, it was not quite in the way that most people do.'

'Why's that?'

He had apparently been thinking about the matter and had his answer ready. 'When I was small she was only one of several people I was dependent on. To use a trendy expression, I "bonded" with my grandmother more than with my mother because she was there all the time. I was quite close to Diane too. She was fourteen when I was born and besotted with babies but she spent time with me later as we both got older. She wasn't always like she is now. She used to draw and paint – and laugh because she was amused rather than just to gush over you.'

'So what changed her?'

Philip sat back to consider. 'I think,' he ventured, after a moment, 'that Diane felt jealous of my mother, though she'd deny it vigorously. Mother amused the parents, was good company without having to try. Diane thought herself ordinary, felt she had to earn approval. It's the general opinion that she married Barry because he's rich, but I think it was because he never expects anything of her. He accepts her and values her as she is. She covered up by pretending to despise my mother and she became more attached to material things. Perhaps she found them less confusing than people.' He blinked. 'What started me on all that?'

'You were telling me why you seem unemotional in the face of your mother's death.'

'So I was.' He was silent for some time and Jennifer waited patiently until he was ready to go on. 'When my mother first met Mark I was angry at having to live with them away from the rest of the family.'

'But you liked Mark?'

'Yes – when I got to know him. It was the same with Nick. He's a good man too. I gave them both hell and by the time I began to value them they'd gone and I couldn't apologize, make up for everything.' His manner became brisk. 'Well, after all that, how can I help?'

Jennifer shrugged. 'Frankly, I don't know. We're doing fine. I just want you to talk. Often, significant details spring out as we find common factors or contradictions in everyone's different versions.'

'It sounds alarming.'

'Only if you've something to hide.'

'I suppose so. Here goes, then.' He began an account of the funeral in all its stages, the gist of which was becoming boringly familiar to Jennifer. His mother's high spirits had offended him. 'In church she sang "Abide With Me" as if she was in the crowd at the Cup Final. Donna was trying not to giggle and Toni was squirming. She says that's ruled St Barnabas' out for our wedding.'

Philip himself had been asked to leave the crematorium promptly so as to be there to welcome any guests who arrived sooner than the dignified progress of the official car brought Diane herself home. As Philip had been in Birmingham on business until late on Monday, Antonia had collected the spare key from Diane the day before and left it in his flat. Considering the number of people his aunt had hired, Philip felt there had been no need for all that but Diane thought that a member of the family should be there to greet the first guest.

His mother had begun drinking immediately. 'You'd have thought that, on this one occasion, she'd have kept off it.'

'But isn't that the point? Her problem was that she couldn't. If she was upset, she'd need a drink even more.'

'Yes, I knew that really. Actually, Grandfather wouldn't have minded. She could do little wrong in his eyes. I was just angry with her for letting herself down.' He considered this judgement for a moment, his eyes on his clasped hands, then he looked at Jennifer. 'I wanted to ask your advice. There's something I'm worried about.'

'Go on then.'

Philip got up and began pacing the floor. 'It's my young

sister. You'll have gathered she loves making a drama and she keeps saying she knows who – well, did the killing. I doubt very much whether she does but whoever it is might not realize that. Can you do anything?'

Jennifer promised to bring the matter to Mitchell's attention.

A key turned in the hall door and Philip answered Jennifer's enquiring glance. 'It's only Toni.'

'She lives here?'

'On and off.'

'According to how you're getting on?'

'According to how she and Daddy are getting on. She's living at her family home at present, unless she's got a suitcase with her now.'

Antonia Grant, empty-handed, burst into the room, then checked as she saw Jennifer. The scratches on her face were already healing. The skin between the thin lines of scarring was no longer inflamed. She gave the sergeant a charm-school smile. 'Shall I go away? I wasn't at this gathering and I've already told my all to an earnest police constable.'

Jennifer remained uncharmed. 'What did your all consist of?'

She dropped to the arm of a chair and pulled her fiancé into it, playing with his hair as she spoke to Jennifer. 'That I work in the export department at Victor Grant, that I'm engaged to Philip Conroy who's being groomed to replace Dad when he retires. That I had to leave the proceedings on Tuesday immediately after the church service, without even attending the crematorium, because I had an appointment with a client who was flying to Australia that evening. That I'd never been in the Bateses' house on any occasion before collecting the key on Monday evening.'

'Did you spend long there?'

'No. I was offered a drink but I'd already had one glass and I was driving. I just went into the hall and Diane produced the key from a drawer in the chest.'

It occurred to Jennifer that Toni probably wished that Diane had been her fiancé's mother. 'And does the rank of detective sergeant merit any additions to what you revealed to your earnest PC?'

She slid into the chair as Philip vacated it. 'Well, I was glad of an excuse to avoid the socializing bit.'

'Because the Bateses aren't your kind of people?'

'Because, except for people who've travelled a long way and have to be fed, the social side of funerals seems to me to be totally out of keeping with the occasion. To appear to be enjoying yourself smacks of lack of feeling for the deceased. To mooch around miserably is to be an ungrateful and impolite guest. Much better to do the church and crem bit and go straight home. I realize that Lorraine and Diane didn't agree with me.'

'Neither,' Philip put in, 'did Edgar.'

When Jennifer returned to the station some time later she found Colin Warren in the foyer again, causing the same disruption to the station routine as he had done on Wednesday. Jennifer was surprised.

'Hey, no one gave you permission to shove your whole workload on to us. Unless you want to do a swap, of course. We'll have the services of your actress and you can remind yourself what real work's like by taking over our case.' When Warren turned, Jennifer saw that he was not amused. 'It's something serious, isn't it? What's happened?'

He scratched his head. 'Well, even if we did swap, you couldn't have my actress. She's gone missing.'

Jennifer whistled. 'You really did have one?'

'I have an amateur one, and very useful she is when she's here.'

Jennifer unlocked the door at the side of the counter that led to the station's nether regions. 'Come upstairs and tell me the whole story. We'll use Benny's office. It's his turn to rot in court this afternoon and we'll be lucky if he's back for the six thirty debriefing.'

She rang for coffee and made the anxious Warren comfortable. 'Now, let's hear it. Vital statistics first.'

Warren still did not smile. 'She was supposed to check in last night and she didn't. Then I rang – several times – but her mobile's always been switched off. She didn't turn up again today. She's only been with me for a week or two, but she seemed sensible and reliable . . .'

Jennifer had her notebook out and her pencil in her hand. 'We'll get there faster if we start at the beginning. What are you currently working on and what, specifically, had you given her to do?'

Warren counted jobs off on his fingers. 'We've just cleared up on finding his birth mother for an adopted boy. The adoptive mother went berserk but I did most of the work on that myself and it was me who got the flak. There's been no trouble with any of the other jobs. We finished the bankruptcy notices as I was telling you yesterday. We're looking into an office theft and she's done two half-days' temping there under an assumed name to see what she could suss out. That was last Thursday and Friday. We're also on two "unfaithful partners" obbos. She's doing one of those, followed the bloke on Monday and should have done the same on Wednesday. She couldn't do Tuesday because she had to go to her father's funeral.'

In their hotel room, Barry and Diane Bates were locked in earnest discussion that was not quite a quarrel. Barry paced the room and gestured energetically to make his points. '. . . and the longer the girl's with us, the longer she has to get used to our lifestyle and the more she's going to look askance at Nick's twopenny-ha'penny set-up in that attic.'

Diane was puzzled. 'You've changed your tune a bit. Yesterday, you were trying to talk me out of offering the child a home. I listened to all your objections, thought seriously about them. We are rather set in our ways to cope with an adolescent girl's irrational behaviour and we would always have Nick breathing down our necks, even if he agreed to the idea at all. Now you're talking as though every objection has been answered.'

'My arguments were driven by what I wanted yesterday. I've had time to sleep on the idea.'

'I did rather spring it on you.'

'You did. Most of my objections aren't insurmountable.'

Resentment replaced the puzzlement. 'You said I wanted a dressed-up daughter as an accessory to my smart outfits. You said I didn't love her!'

He saw with compunction that his remarks of the previous day had upset her more than he had intended. He tried a grin. 'I know, and I'm sorry. You know I overstate when I want my own way. I think I misjudged you.'

'You're talking nonsense, Barry. You never overstate your case. That's why I hardly ever argue with you. Your deadly logic is always unanswerable. Anyway, you didn't misjudge Nick. That's what convinced me to give up the idea. Nick will never give up his claim, and, in court, he'd win hands down.'

Barry stopped pacing and stood, silhouetted against the window. 'So, we'll do it by gentle persuasion – show Donna the good life. Surely she deserves a bit of that. When we've convinced her that we're her best bet, then we'll have a lever with Nick. He'd agree to anything if it was what Donna really wanted.'

She shook her head. 'You're repeating my arguments to you yesterday. Come on, why have you changed your mind? You were dead set against it yesterday. I didn't think you were even listening to me. What's different today?'

He told her.

'My God, Barry!' She sank on to the bed, her head in her hands. 'How long have you known? Will you ever forgive me? What are we going to do now?'

She shook her head, expecting no answers. When he came to her, she accepted his arms round her shoulders without bridling, let his persuasive tone and practical suggestions soothe her. 'We're going to stick together. We're going to pull ourselves together. We're going to do our duty together to the remainder of the family. We'll give Lorraine's daughter a proper home and put right the things we can, as we're able.'

'I can't put right what I've done.'

He kissed her, smudging her lipstick. She did not leap up to repair it. Tears welled, ran down her cheeks and did further damage to her mask of cosmetics. They sat together until they were relatively calm again.

Donna was pleased when her aunt told her that they would not be sleeping at this hotel any more. She packed her bag obediently and cheerfully. At first she had enjoyed the novelty and luxury, not having to help with the dishes and having her own choice of breakfast and supper dishes.

Midday picnics in Dad's room had been more fun though. Dad would have to go back to school soon and he said she must too. She didn't mind. She liked school. She stowed her belongings away neatly as she made plans. If Dad was teaching all day, he must have the bed and she'd sleep on the inflatable mattress on the floor till the police had finished with Dad's house.

She wouldn't mention that to Auntie Di though or she'd offer to have them both to stay till things were settled. That wouldn't be as good as having Dad all to herself. Anyway, Auntie Di wouldn't really want them. She just wouldn't want neighbours to say, 'You would have thought their rich relations would have taken care of them.'

Donna was sorry for her aunt. She was never happy until everyone was impressed with her or thought well of her. Donna had decided long ago that it was easier to please one person and the one might just as well be herself. That didn't stop her trying to do what Dad and Mum wanted, and Miss Gladwin, her English teacher, or even, sometimes, Philip. But it didn't go as far as the silly Bateses or stuck up Antonia Grant.

Actually, she seemed to have the knack of pleasing her

aunt without really trying. She was quiet and neat and tidy and that suited most grown-ups. At home with Mum, it had been the only way to be. Life would have been completely chaotic if both of them had scattered possessions around and generally created mayhem.

She closed the bag's zip over her carefully folded clothes and sat on the bed. She would probably have half an hour to herself now. Her aunt had brought clothes enough for a month and her packing would be a major operation. At least she hadn't dragged Uncle Barry off to the dance in the hotel ballroom last night but she had gone down to dinner in full regalia, to borrow an expression of Dad's, twittering about keeping up appearances.

Donna dug her diary out of the side pocket of the holdall, turned to the current page and began to write. It was some time afterwards that a tap came at the door. Donna stuffed the diary away before calling to her visitor to come in.

Her uncle appeared. 'All set for Elm Road?'

Donna frowned. 'Isn't Dad collecting me from here?'

'Collecting you?' Donna began to feel uneasy. 'You'd better see your aunt about that. Anyway, if he is coming, you might as well be settling in while you wait.'

Donna sat back on the bed beside her bag, partly because her legs were trembling and partly as a gesture of defiance. Her aunt appeared behind her uncle in the doorway. 'Settling in where? Not at Elm Road.'

Barry looked nonplussed but Diane thought she understood the problem. 'You won't be having the spare room where your mum died. Uncle Barry will take that for his study and you can have the study as your room.'

Donna's heart sank but she remained polite. Perhaps Dad had agreed to this arrangement until they could have his house back. She felt rather miffed that he hadn't mentioned it to her but she supposed he had a lot on his mind. She nodded slowly. 'The police won't be long with our house, will they?'

'You mean your mother's house? I don't know.' She

looked across at her husband. 'I suppose it might revert to him.'

Donna was bewildered. 'But we'll be living in it, Dad and I.'

'Don't be silly, Donna, you can't live with your father. You're not old enough to keep house and an impractical man like Nick won't be any good at it. Look at his set-up in Victoria Road! Don't worry, dear. You'll always have a home with us and you'll probably see more of your father than you did before.'

'But Dad . . .'

Barry added his support. 'Your father quite agrees with us. We discussed it last night.'

Donna had thought, when her mother died, that she had already experienced abandon. Now she knew what that was really like. There were no tears. She was well rehearsed in covering her feelings and getting on with what had to be done.

Diane was doing her best. Now she made the supreme sacrifice. 'We'll all go to McDonald's later to cheer you up. It's time I had another burger. The last time I had one I was about your age.'

Donna was making lightning plans. She nodded. 'Are you taking the things down to the car? I need the loo. I'll come down in a minute.'

Barry lifted the holdall. 'We needn't get a porter just for this. I'll carry it down.'

Diane, with a warning to Donna not to be long, checked her two vanity cases and the various small items she preferred to keep personal charge of and followed her husband to the lift. Donna sat on the bed and counted slowly to thirty before she emerged into the corridor.

Jennifer was staring at Warren across Mitchell's desk. 'Don't you read the papers, man?'

'When I've time. What have I missed?'

Jennifer scrabbled in her case and produced the previous day's *Clarion*. She pushed it across for Warren to read the article she indicated. His eyes widened. 'This was Lorraine? I do remember skimming through the piece but it calls her Conroy. She calls herself Felling.'

'Yes, she did.' Briefly, Jennifer explained the present state of the police's case to her shocked listener. 'You've already explained one little mystery for us. Working for you was presumably the new job that Lorraine was muttering about when she was being helped upstairs.'

'Helped?'

'She was legless.'

Warren shook his head. 'I didn't know she drank.'

'Really?' Jennifer was surprised. 'Maybe she only needed to resort to it when she had the family to face.'

Warren became businesslike. 'This chap she was following – you'll want to know about him.' Jennifer's answer was to pick up her notebook again. 'He wasn't an "errant husband", actually – more of a toy-boy. Our client had been living with him. She's a woman of about forty and she thought he had taken up with someone more his own age. Who could blame him? But we only have to do what the client pays for, so long as it's legal.

'It was the usual story, the odd phone call when the receiver was put down immediately the woman answered, a few evening absences that he didn't have a good enough explanation for – and so on. She said she didn't want to spoil things by accusing him but she had to know . . .' Warren stopped speaking and Jennifer suspected he was blaming himself for putting his assistant at risk.

'Lorraine's daughter was spending the weekend with her father and she was at school on the Monday so she was free to follow him. Twice he sneaked away from the love nest and both times it was a man he met, not a girl. The two of them talked for a bit. An envelope was handed over discreetly and the older man wrote something in a notebook. It seemed to be information from the younger man. It's not funny in the circumstances, but we had a laugh about it on Monday evening.'

'What was the joke?'

'Well, Lorraine knew the man.' Jennifer blinked in confusion and Warren paused to clarify. 'The toy-boy, Craig, met an older man who was a friend, or at least an acquaintance of Lorraine's. She'd spent the weekend padded out as a stout middle-aged woman in a headscarf and got away with that. On Monday, though, she was almost certain the older man saw and recognized her . . .'

'Would it matter?'

'Well, it would have been thought odd. She was got up as . . . well, a bit different from how she presented herself to meet this chap normally.'

Jennifer's mind was turning somersaults. Warren raised an eyebrow in enquiry.

'I don't suppose his name is Neville Scott?'

'How did you know?'

Jennifer explained, ending his story with the consultant's unauthorized trip to Saudi Arabia. 'So, what did he hand over to your client's boyfriend? Drugs? Blackmail money?'

Warren shrugged. 'Could be anything. I told you. This was last Monday. I never saw her again so it had gone no further. We'd discussed swapping jobs in case Lorraine had been rumbled. If she'd been in ordinary dress there would have been no reason why she shouldn't just be having a drink in the same pub but he must have thought it was very strange to see her all done up as she was, looking dowdy and double her usual figure. So, what now?'

Jennifer was already making a list. 'We'll have someone meeting his return flight. If he isn't on it we start international negotiations. In the meantime, I ask Lorraine's sister if Scott was invited to the after-funeral party as he claims or whether he invited himself. It would be easy to put a well-mannered, middle-class woman like Diane into a position where she was obliged to ask him.'

The telephone on Mitchell's desk rang and Jennifer lifted the receiver. She listened for a few seconds, replied, 'I'm on my way,' and gathered her possessions. Excusing herself to Warren, she explained, 'If you want to stay in on this, unofficially, we'll be back here at six thirty. In the meantime, as you heard, I've got to go.'

Mr Denby was enjoying his moment of glory with Beardsmore. He had described all the fine shades of subtlety in Edgar's fork attack and his discovered check, and his own defences against these devilish wiles.

He had been persuaded to digress into all the details of the various relationships within the Smith, Conroy and Felling families and the events of Tuesday afternoon.

'Apple of his eye, was young Lorraine, because she refused to let anything pull her down. There was only one thing he said he would never forgive her for and that was producing young Philip. It wasn't the scandal, mind you.' The old man paused and chuckled bronchitically. 'What annoyed Edgar was being made a grandfather so early. Said it got him labelled an old man before he'd half finished his youth.' Another chuckle brought on a major coughing fit and Beardsmore wondered how long it would be before Mr Denby and Edgar Smith were poring together over a chessboard again in the great beyond.

'Was there some reason why he didn't get on with his younger daughter?'

Mr Denby was indignant. 'Who told you that? He got on with all the family. It was just that he thought Lorraine had kept the old spirit alive.' He saw that Beardsmore looked puzzled. 'Edgar came from nowhere. Brought up in a back street, started as the boy who swept the floor and made the tea. He wasn't work-shy and he wanted to learn engineering. It fascinated him.'

'A self-made man, was he?'

'Don't know about that. He enjoyed his working-class childhood. He wasn't one o' these social climbers. He just loved solving engineering puzzles, I think. May was different. She was thrilled when they got well off and could afford nice things She learned to talk with a fancy accent and to "fit in". Edgar called a spade a bloody shovel to his dying day.'

'And Diane was like her mother?' Beardsmore had to wait for Mr Denby to catch his breath.

'S'right. But Lorraine was a back-street kid, had no time for airs and graces. Diane had riding lessons and a pony of her own. Lorraine said she'd have a horse when she'd a cart for it to pull. She could see the riding was only for keeping up with the Joneses. Lorraine did like animals. She loved the little mongrel pup she bought from the animal shelter with the pocket money she'd saved. Edgar made her pay for its food out of her own money, to teach her a sense of responsibility. Not sure that experiment worked.' He choked again, alarmingly, before adding, 'Edgar paid the vet's bills. He wasn't unreasonable, just didn't want the girls spoilt, but May used to work against him.'

'It seems strange he left her all that money then.'

'Nah! He said she was the only one who knew how to enjoy it. And there were two children to think about.'

This seemed a little inconsistent to Beardsmore. 'I'd have thought he'd want his grandchildren to succeed by their own efforts, considering what you've said.'

The old man shook his head. 'He wasn't the first silly sod to be softer on his grandchildren than he was on his children. Besides, the chances were that Lorraine would have spent most of it by the time she popped off. No one thought about it ending like this. Thought I'd be dead and gone long before either of 'em.'

Since there was nothing to reply to this, Beardsmore merely nodded and the old man sat musing and wheezing. After a moment he looked up. 'There was Nick, of course. He made his house over to Lorraine when they split up so that the girl would always have a roof over her head. Pretty generous really when you consider the lass was the one who threw him out. Edgar wanted him to put some bar on her selling it but he wouldn't. That's why Edgar left Nick the value of the house in cash. He didn't think Nick should have to suffer, though he did think he was a bit of a fool to back out and let Lorraine have things all her own way.'

'Why do you think he did?'

'Who knows? Anyway, he'll get it now.'

'Are you telling me Lorraine left a will benefiting Nicholas Felling?'

'Well, of course she did. She knew he'd look after Donna and that way Antonia Grant wouldn't get any of it through Philip.'

'She didn't approve of her son's choice of wife?'

Mr Denby gave a shout of laughter. 'She called her "that trollop"! That's rich, isn't it, coming from Lorraine?'

It had been just a stroke of luck that Shakila had heard her relations discussing their friend who had been burgled during his wife's funeral. It had not been lucky for the victim, of course. Perhaps Shakila could claim a morsel of credit for remembering the incident when it became relevant to her case and the rest had followed. She, and the computer, had discovered the florist as the link between the burglaries and now she was on her way to follow him up. At the very least she was being trusted to investigate a series of burglaries and at best she might apprehend a murderer.

Shakila found Adam Flowers not nearly so co-operative as the funeral directors. It seemed not a very appropriate name for the red-faced, harsh-voiced manager of the large shop. She felt the atmosphere cold and damp as she entered. Real flowers, she realized, would not thrive in heat and dryness. She pitied the two assistants with their blue-red fingers and pinched faces.

The younger of them, a thin girl with a ponytail, had taken a look at the proffered warrant card and gone to speak to her employer. The voice, high-pitched, could be heard in the shop. '. . . a police officer! It's a woman and she's black!'

Shakila had been grudgingly taken into the office at the back of the shop. It was considerably less opulent than the front and Shakila found the little cubicle, though not the company, less offensive. It was apparent to her that there was not much chance of obtaining her interviewee's good will. 'What happens,' she enquired, without any preamble, 'when you're called in by one of your contracted funeral directors?'

Mr Flowers glared. 'Why do you want to know?'

'You've got an objection to telling me? It's a fairly straightforward question.'

'All right. We're given all the details of the ceremonies at the church or crematorium, the times and the requirements in the way of flowers and greenery. We have to liaise with the vicars and other officials about when the places are free for us to go in. Usually, it's Doreen who arranges them. She's got a diploma for it.'

'So she runs that side of the business?'

He bridled. 'I run the business. Doreen puts the flowers in vases or does pedestal arrangements and wreaths. John delivers them. Gail stays here and looks after the shop.'

'And what do you do?'

Mr Flowers' face darkened angrily. 'What do you think I do? Go round burgling all the houses while the mourners are safely out of the way?' Shakila's jaw dropped and Flowers stared at her. 'Bloody hell! Is that what this is all about? I can give you your man right now, and when you go and get him, tell him not to come back here if he wants to keep his head on his shoulders!'

Suddenly, Mr Flowers was anxious to be of all the help he could. It was the last time he would ever give anyone a second chance. It was only because he was a friend of Gail's and she had assured him that Kennedy had been the stooge for a more slippery customer.

Shakila listened to the story of John Kennedy's previous conviction and Mr Flowers' noble attempt to help him back on to the straight and narrow by giving him a job. 'I kept him on the vans where he wasn't being tempted by handling money.'

'That was noble of you. I expect you paid him a decent salary so that he had no need to revert to his criminal activities.'

Flowers' face was turning from blotchy red to an unhealthy purple. 'He couldn't expect the going rate with a record. He'd have had his rise if he'd proved himself . . .'

Shakila collected details of Kennedy's home address and his work schedule for the day and escaped thankfully from Mr Flowers' unpleasant company. As she set off for the block of flats where Kennedy lived with his mother, she searched her memory. Someone at the station had mentioned that name before in the last few days.

Chapter Seven

Mitchell's briefing on Thursday evening was short and his mannner urgent. Before he began to speak he placed a small book on the desk in front of him. It had cartoon animals drawn on it in bright colours. For once he gave the team little chance to speak, summarizing each member's new information for the benefit of the rest and inviting no comment. They all knew that, at this point, action was more important than discussion.

'You'll all know by now about the missing child.' He described briefly how Donna had made an excuse to remain behind in her hotel room after her aunt and uncle went down to load their car. 'Her uncle is convinced she's run away. Her aunt thinks she's been abducted with her father as favourite suspect.

'There's an army of men out already, doing all the usual things. Jennifer, take a PC and see the school people. Find out who her special friends are and follow them up too. There are more men available if you think you need them. Caroline, take Beardsmore and see Philip Conroy and Antonia Grant. Find out if the child has confided anything to them.'

Mitchell gave out the rest of his action sheets, sending officers to interview hotel staff and to the hospital to make discreet enquiries about any aspects of the career of Neville Scott that he had not been willing to reveal himself. He had curtly acknowledged Warren's presence as he came in and he now explained his connection with their enquiry.

'All the other aspects of the case are just as important

114

as before. Mr Denby hasn't told us any more about the family's financial arrangements than we knew from the solicitor. What's important is that he seems not to have felt any necessity to keep the facts to himself and it is therefore likely that all beneficiaries of either will would know the score. There's a lot of money involved but we mustn't confine ourselves to considering the people who inherit large sums. People have been killed for the sake of quite minor bequests. Under Lorraine's will, a large sum is left to Nicholas Felling, but money has been left in modest amounts to Philip Conroy, the Bateses and various friends and good causes. The details are all in here.' He laid his hand on the file.

'If you've read all the reports in here as thoroughly as you should, you'll realize that the girl has been making claims to know who killed her mother. You'll also realize that she's the sort of child it's dangerous to believe. However, whoever is guilty of this crime may not be willing to take the risk. We need to find Donna quickly. The little book is Donna's diary. I intend to have some passages photocopied for you all to see. The diary was in the side pocket of the holdall that she packed and that Barry Bates took away.'

'She was probably counting on being expected to carry it down herself. She wouldn't have wanted to run off with nothing to wear besides what she had on.'

'At least she'd have taken the diary if she had the chance. I wouldn't have dared let anyone see mine when I was thirteen.'

Mitchell held up a hand. 'Sorry, but I can't let you speculate till later. There's too much to be done. I've almost finished. There's a little bit more from Dr Holland. The scrapings from Lorraine's nails were found to be fragments of her own skin as she tried to push the pillow away from her face and neck.

'There won't be another briefing until eight thirty in the morning. Try to keep going tonight till all your actions are completed. My mobile number's on all your sheets. Check in with me before going off duty. Good luck.'

115

Alone again, he leafed through the diary once more, certain that it contained the clues they needed. The entries varied through wishful thinking, fantasy and bald statement to honest outpourings of feelings that were too much for a child to contain. Much of this related to her mother. The girl was very articulate, but then, she was the daughter of an English teacher.

Mitchell began to read again the passage that had struck him most forcibly on first perusal. 'If only she could have been someone else's mother. Then I'd have thought she was wonderful, envied the someone else for having such a with-it parent. Having to live with her makes me cross and sometimes frightened. She doesn't give a toss what anybody thinks about her.'

On another page, Donna described a conversation she had had with her mother on the subject of Antonia Grant. 'Mum says it's a mother's duty to get on with her daughter-in-law. I don't see why, especially if she's as horrible as Ant Grant. I think having her in the family will spoil it. I hate her and I might kill her.' Was the child serious? The lead-up to this melodramatic statement had been sensible enough. Of course, all adolescents were moody and Donna seemed to be more mercurial than most.

The only entry for the previous Tuesday read, 'My mother was killed today. I know who did it but no one will believe me.'

Mitchell suddenly remembered that Donna had lost her diary at her aunt's house on Tuesday and her father had found it. He said that he had assured her that he had not read it. Would he have been able to resist that peep into the private life of a daughter whose company he was often denied? There were a lot of reasons for taking another hard look at Felling. He had been having to live in a poky flat to keep up his maintenance payments. He had owned a surprisingly spacious house in a pleasant area of town before making it over to his partner because she had custody of his daughter. He must have been furious to see the money he handed over being spent on the drink that made his ex-partner a laughing stock and laid on Donna the sort of burden no thirteen-year-old should have to carry.

Mitchell smiled to himself. Giving the same suspect three different motives for murder smacked of harassment.

Nicholas Felling, sitting beside his telephone in case his daughter, or her abductor, tried to get in touch with him, was not pleased to see Clement. He was even more affronted when his visitor demanded an account of how he had spent his afternoon.

He gave it resentfully. He had been in school, teaching his normal timetable until three fifty when the school day ended. 'We all snatched a coffee and trooped to the library for the monthly staff meeting. It went on till after five. Don't ask me what happened in it. It's always mind-numbingly tedious and I wasn't feeling madly interested in school affairs to begin with. I was worrying about Donna, about what more I could have done for Lorraine . . .' He gestured helplessness with his hands. 'I'd have done better to have cut the meeting and gone to fetch her as soon as I was free, but I thought it was time I was back at work. I didn't want to start off Donna's new regime with social workers hovering over us because I'd been sacked.'

He shook his head as if to clear it. 'Of course, I'd probably be able to retire, once all the legal matters are sorted out. I haven't taken in that I'm about to be rich. It's not the sort of thing a schoolmaster is adapted to. Anyway, it wouldn't be good for us to be the idle rich. That's not the sort of future I see for either of us. If we have a future at all.'

The panic had returned to his face. He stared at the phone, willing it to ring, then returned his gaze to Clement. 'Why was I not informed immediately . . .?'

'But you were. At least as soon as we knew ourselves. Donna disappeared from the hotel just after lunch. I suppose your sister-in-law, knowing Donna's love of melodrama, wanted to give her time to finish her little protest against authority without anyone else having to worry about it. When they realized her absence could be a serious matter –'

'Could be serious! What the hell –'

Clement's voice was soothing. 'Mr Felling, we've got half the West Yorkshire force out there, looking for your daughter. We couldn't be taking her disappearance more seriously. At the same time, there's a chance she's holed up somewhere, quite safe, either enjoying the excitement, or, more likely, feeling bereft and bewildered and unable to face the stress of yet another change of circumstances – but physically safe, nonetheless.'

Felling nodded and appeared slightly calmer. 'So why are you wanting my movements?'

'Simply to eliminate you from the list of people who might be responsible.'

'But why should I have to resort to cloak and dagger tactics? I shall have custody without question now.'

'Your sister-in-law believes otherwise. She went so far as to tell Donna that, after some discussion with you, it had been decided that she should remain at Elm Road.'

Felling let out a roar of rage that surprised both of them, himself particularly. 'Well, now we know why she's gone.' He sat silent for several moments, breathing heavily. He spoke again when he had himself in hand. 'I'm very angry at what you've just told me, but very relieved too.'

'Are you saying that no such conversation took place?'

'I'm saying that Diane, for some unknown reason, has twisted my thanks for the good care she's taken of my daughter this week, and a few remarks about having to smarten up my slapdash bachelor ways. I was trying to please her when I said that, if I wasn't careful, I'd have Donna wishing she was back in the civilized comfort of Elm Road.'

'And she misunderstood you.'

'Of course she didn't!' He put his head in his hands and spoke to Clement through his fingers. 'I couldn't think of any reason why Donna should take off. We'd made our

118

plans. If she thought I'd let Diane talk me out of them, she'd . . .' He put his hands down again in an appeal to Clement. 'Can you imagine what she's going through?'

Not more than the man in front of him, Clement decided.

Mitchell's phone gave a welcome ring that rescued him from the case's mountain of paperwork.

'It's Shakila, sir. I've been up to the Infirmary. I saw that theatre nurse again and one of the other consultants. They told me quite a lot about Mr Scott but I'm not sure that any of it is relevant to the enquiry. They laugh at his mannerisms a bit, but he seems to be well liked and respected. He was the youngest man in this authority ever to get a consultancy but he never fulfilled his early promise because of his wife.'

'His wife?'

'When he was still a student, he married a young tennis player who was on the verge of going professional. Within a couple of years of getting married she had to drop out of the game because she was found to be suffering from Addison's disease.'

'What's that?'

'It's a wasting disease, according to the nurse. Your muscles become useless. Must have been hell for an athlete. It wasn't Scott's line at all but naturally he read it up and found out all he could and the next thing anybody knew he had set up a small research team at his own expense, working from some hospital in Leeds. Meanwhile he was looking after his wife at home with the help of domestics and a nurse. Now she's in a nursing home, that one at Meadowbank near where the Bateses live.

'I'd guess the nurse is his bit on the side. I suppose he deserves some pleasure. Anyway, if she isn't, then I think she'd like to be. She's heard that one of the team has come up with a new compound that Scott thinks will help his wife but all the clinical trials will take time, which she hasn't got.'

119

Mitchell had scribbled notes throughout the call. He slipped them into the file. 'Well done, Shakila. Get that written up, then you can knock off.'

'With luck,' Caroline remarked to Beardsmore as they rang Philip Conroy's doorbell, 'we shall find the love birds together and be saved a journey.'

Beardsmore was not so sure that seeing the two together was the best way of getting the information they needed. Voices could be heard as an internal door opened and Philip came down the hall to let them in. His visitor proved to be not Antonia but her father.

They all shook hands as though the officers were invited guests and Beardsmore was surprised to see Caroline accept a glass of wine, even more surprised when she nodded her agreement to his accepting one for himself too. Having established the atmosphere of an informal party, Philip looked affronted when Caroline produced not a conversational platitude but a blunt question. 'Have you any idea where your sister might be?'

He shook his head. 'I daren't think. I told the other officer I was afraid for her because of the claims she was making. I've driven round the streets looking for her, I've phoned all her friends' parents but some of them aren't home yet. I don't know what to do now so I'm getting drunk.' His distress seemed quite genuine to Beardsmore.

Victor Grant said, apologetically, 'I'm afraid I brought the wine. I didn't know about Donna until I got here. What I did know was that, after more than six months of playing games with Phil, my infuriating daughter has at long last consented to name the day. I came to give my fatherly blessing and congratulate him. It seemed a good excuse for cracking a vintage bottle.'

'But Antonia didn't come with you?'

Grant laughed. 'I came because she's away. There wouldn't have been much chance of a man-to-man chat with her around.'

'So, she doesn't know that Donna's missing?'

Grant blinked. 'I don't know. Probably not. She's over in Manchester to see a show that an actress friend of hers is in. She's staying at the Metropole for the night. She's giving herself a treat for her successful lunch with Mr Shute.' Meeting Caroline's enquiring look, he explained. 'He's a wool merchant. Australian. Charming man but he drives a mean bargain. Toni had her meal with him on Tuesday and wound him round her little finger. She brought off a deal better than I'd dreamed of. He went off to catch his afternoon flight to Sydney thinking we'd done him a favour. Do you need to see her? I'll get her to contact you as soon as she gets back. Or you could reach her at the hotel after about half eleven.'

Caroline turned back to Philip who was looking startled. 'Mr Conroy, if someone has abducted your sister, then the onus in the search is on our police machine. If, however, she has run away, for whatever reason, then we need her family, who know her best, to help us. How likely –'

'Very likely,' Philip cut in, 'if she decided it would be an interesting thing to do, though she's never done it before.'

'And you've no idea where she might go?'

Philip sighed and further disarranged his rumpled hair. 'I've told you. I've rung her friends already.' He brightened. 'Have you tried Mr Denby?'

Caroline shook her head. 'No, we haven't. Good thinking. Or, is there any chance . . . well, some reason Antonia might be hiding her?'

'Whatever would Toni have to gain –'

'You misunderstand me, Mr Grant. Would Donna have run to Antonia from whatever has upset her?'

Philip shrugged. 'Vic's just said. She isn't there to run to. Besides, they didn't get on at all. Donna says Toni's stuck up and Toni thinks Donna's a spoilt brat. They're both only half right. Maybe the prospect of being a bridesmaid will bring Donna round.'

'She can't be a bridesmaid until we've found her,' Victor Grant pointed out reasonably.

'I gather you weren't at Edgar Smith's funeral, Mr Grant.'

There was a silence as they all stared at Beardsmore. Grant looked at Caroline as though waiting for her to reprimand her constable. When she did not, he answered the implied question. 'I was still in Hanover on Tuesday – didn't get back till Wednesday morning. I tried to get an earlier flight but it was impossible. Pity. I'd have liked to pay my respects.'

'Perhaps for the record you could tell us how each of you spent this afternoon.'

They complied with no hesitation. They had been together, 'at the firm', from two o'clock until almost four. One of the secretaries had brought coffee to them at some point. Philip had answered the telephone several times and was willing to identify his callers. Two of them had also spoken to Victor Grant before they rang off. It all seemed quite plausible.

After another few minutes it had become obvious to the two officers that no more useful information would be offered here and they took their leave. Back in the car, Beardsmore asked curiously, 'Did you have a drink with them because you thought it would make them a bit more forthcoming?'

Caroline smiled sweetly. 'No, but thanks for giving me an excuse to offer the CI when I give him our squiffy report.'

Colin Warren's client was beginning to wish she had kept her suspicions about the faithfulness of her new young partner to herself. She was very glad that he had apparently not found himself a new and younger lady friend, but now he was furious with her for not trusting him and she seemed to have got him into trouble with the police. She had never dreamed he would be so silly as to get involved with a coke or crack dealer or she'd have done her best to get him out of it. She'd never have gone to the police, though, and now Mr Warren had stirred up a lot of trouble. When Craig had refused to answer the questions of the young officer who'd called at teatime, he had been taken down to the station. Now, she didn't know when, or even if, she would see him again.

DC Shakila Nazir was trying to cheer herself up. She was sitting in the canteen over a cup of coffee. It was legitimate this time, so that, if the superintendent came in again, after a polite 'Sir' she could continue enjoying her snack. The comfortable fug around her had restored feeling to her hands and feet. Condensation on the window shut out the view and she felt she was in a capsule of human exhaustion as officers came in and went out, nodding or raising a hand in greeting but too tired to make conversation.

It didn't matter to Shakila. She had plenty to say to herself. If someone had told her a week ago that she would have solved a troublesome series of burglaries almost single-handed, she would have been in transports of delight. It was silly, therefore, she told herself sternly, to be disappointed because her villain had not turned out to be a murderer.

At first, Kennedy had denied the burglaries. However, the evidence of his distraught mother and the discovery of Diane Bates's Fabergé egg in his bedroom had rendered his protests vain. The more serious suggestion that he might have suffocated Lorraine Felling in order to facilitate his escape, he had vehemently denied. A uniformed officer, sent to check his account of his subsequent actions, had had it confirmed in all its details. Kennedy had arrived at St Thomas's church where Doreen Wilkes had been waiting for him no more than ten minutes after Lorraine had been tucked into her sister's spare bed.

Shakila had suggested that Miss Wilkes might be Kennedy's accomplice but her account was backed up by the Reverend John Arthurs. The vicar had seen a traffic warden giving Kennedy a ticket. The time on it meant that Kennedy could not possibly have returned to Elm Road before Lorraine's death had been discovered.

Shakila's vision of a banner headline in the *Clarion*, 'DC of less than two years' service solves murder case', faded.

Only half a mile away, in the *Clarion*'s main office, a reporter was already preparing for the following week's edition. He had collected his thoughts under the heading 'Namesake of former US President arrested for funeral burglaries'. His article made no reference to the arresting officer.

Donna Felling had seldom used a public telephone so she was relieved to find clear instructions to users on a disc fastened to the wall. She counted out the coins she would need, thankful that her purse at least had been in her pocket and not tucked into the bag that her uncle had carried away.

She felt nervous. The four glass walls of the kiosk seemed little protection against that gang of yobbos gathered outside the shops further up the road. They'd called out to her as she'd passed them and she'd given them what she hoped was a friendly grin. She wished now that she'd used the phone in Debbie's flat but Mrs Collins would have listened in. She wouldn't have been able to help it, the flat was so small.

The yobs were pushing somebody around now, a girl a bit older than herself. She wondered why they had not interfered with her and suspected it was because they knew she was Debbie's friend. When they'd walked past the gang earlier, Debs had given them a load of cheek and they had all laughed but not in the jeering way they were doing now at this other poor girl they were picking on as she tried to avoid them.

The one called Jonno had terrified her when she had first seen him with his half-shaved head and the weird purple tuft waving about on top. She had tried to count his row of earrings but he kept moving his head before she'd finished. There were more than ten anyway. He had huge boots and a loud voice and used dreadful language.

Debbie said he was ten pence short of a pound and harmless and that the real villain was the ordinary-looking one they called Shaun. His hair was longish and messy but still its natural brown. Debbie said his real dad and all his uncles were in Armley jail and that Shaun carried a knife. Donna could believe it.

She put a twenty-pence coin into the slot in front of her and punched the buttons. The number rang out at the other end twice, then a voice said, 'Hello?' Donna was not pleased. 'I didn't expect it would be you . . . Yes, of course it's me . . . No, it's all right, as long as you'll help.' Donna explained her requirements. 'Just put them in a plastic bag. . . . Yes, thank you . . . I'll wait on the corner, outside the RSPCA. You won't tell anyone, will you? And please don't be long, will you? It's a bit dark and quiet.' She decided not to mention the yobbos, who had let the girl go now and were lighting up whatever stuff it was that they smoked.

Donna came out of the telephone box, wrapping the baggy anorak Debbie had lent her more closely around her thin body. She was thankful that the gang of boys in the precinct seemed to be busy now with some mischief of their own which had no connection with her. She turned her back on them to walk away from the shops towards the corner of the road where the RSPCA building stood in its big scruffy yard.

She wished she had thought of a better place to meet. There would be no one walking a dog or exercising any other animal across there at this hour. Anyone moving about in the yard now would probably be up to no good. Still, the car should be here in a few minutes and then she would have warm things to put on to run round to Debbie's tiny, messy but friendly flat.

She was less hopeful than Debbie that she would get back in without Mrs Collins seeing her. And if she did, would she be returned to either the police or her home? She didn't think Mrs Collins would care much who Debbie had brought home so long as they weren't in her way – and, in any case, it wouldn't matter if she did. She'd have made her point by then. Her father would have realized that she refused to be dumped on her aunt.

She jumped as an eerie wail echoed round her. Then, fiercely, she told herself to be sensible. There were lost dogs in the pound at the back of the building across the road, all just as anxious to be claimed by their rightful owners as she was herself.

After what seemed like an hour, she saw a car approaching. It wasn't the right one, though. She would recognize it even in the dark because of the way its lights were set. This one was too small. She was startled by the way it was being driven, a bit faster than was really safe. She had stepped to the edge of the kerb, ready to take her bag of belongings quickly from the driver. She tried to move back but the vehicle came towards her without losing speed and she stayed rooted to the spot more in astonishment than fear.

Although she knew it was speeding, the car seemed to take an age to reach her. When it hit her, she felt herself floating slowly upwards for a while, and then gently down until the top corner of the roof caught her another blow. After that, she knew nothing.

Chapter Eight

Mitchell was grimly amused. He had to spend his evening at his desk, concentrating on his hated paperwork, his teeth gritted, his thoughts often straying to the more exciting doings of his team. As they checked in, their interruptions as welcome as their information, they apologized as though they were spoiling his pleasure.

Jennifer's knock was particularly welcome. She had traced Donna's headmaster, Malcolm Hill, to a Rotary dinner, where her interruption of his wining and dining had been contrastingly unwelcome. Jennifer seemed not to have been impressed by him. 'Wanted to know if I couldn't have waited at least until the meal was finished. He couldn't place Donna at all at first. When I said she was thirteen, he managed to "remember" that she was in Year 9. He leered at me and started a diatribe on the evils of a system that loaded him with paperwork when he'd rather be getting to know his pupils.'

Mitchell nodded. 'I've met the type. So, you've not got much?'

'On the contrary! He put himself out to the extent of producing the telephone number of Donna's head of year, chiefly as the best and quickest way of getting rid of me. I hope he has the mother and father of a hangover tomorrow.'

'So, you hunted out his colleague? Any good?'

Jennifer made herself as comfortable as she could on a chair with sagging upholstery. 'A definite improvement. While being strictly professional, she made it clear that she shared my opinion of her boss. She said a lot about

127

Donna's English work and her imagination – didn't seem surprised that her diary contained some weird items and a lot of wishful thinking. She says it's not uncommon for adolescent girls who are good on the arts side – although Donna's not a star pupil academically.

'When she couldn't tell me anything else, she took me along to a house nearby where one of Donna's friends lived. The mother was anxious to oblige Miss Vardy, but Rachel, the girl, wasn't helpful. She just kept saying she hadn't known Donna was going to disappear and she had no idea where she might have gone. She told me Donna was always saying she'd run away, but no one had taken any notice. I asked why and she said, "She couldn't, could she? Who'd look after her mum?"'

Mitchell raised his eyebrows and said, 'Quite.'

Caroline, back home from her interview with Philip Conroy, had checked in with Mitchell by telephone. She could not understand why, with their case at a critical stage, a murderer unidentified and a child either run away or abducted, her thoughts insisted on returning to her own past. Maybe it was lack of sleep over the last few days that was causing her to move from task to task like an automaton, the set routine of an investigation dictating the next move rather than her own thinking.

She had come by a circuitous route to her present position. Her three years at the Royal Northern College of Music, studying piano and singing, had been abandoned just as performing opportunities and offers began to come in. She had found the concert platform and hotel life lonely, and performing to a large, paying audience less satisfying than playing amongst amateurs and friends. It was tedious too to have to worry about the professional critics who could make or mar her career and whose opinions she didn't always respect. It was not sour grapes – the critics had been kind to her – but the musical fellowship was missing in a solo career. Caroline had little personal vanity and even less material ambition. For a short while she had considered teaching music but had applied to the force on a whim and never regretted it. She had particularly enjoyed her work since transferring to CID. She realized that she had had more credibility as a detective since the job had ruined her face and she felt less bitterness about this than her colleagues thought.

Suddenly, and for the first time, it occurred to her to wonder how her husband felt about her disfigurement. It had never been discussed between them, apart from the medical aspects at the time of the attack and just afterwards. She had refused cosmetic as opposed to necessary surgery so far, preferring to see how tidily her wounds would heal with time. The longer that time went on, the more used she grew to her new face – not that she had much time to spare for either looking at or thinking about it.

Would Cavill prefer her patched up more completely? She thought it concerned him as little as it did herself and she wouldn't insult him by asking if her scars altered his feelings.

Now she needed some music, but she was too tired to play herself and too afraid of stirring regrets to listen to piano music played by a professional. She decided that Richard Strauss's *Four Last Songs* would suit the moment and slipped the disc into the machine. Someone had once told her that Strauss had composed his first song, a Christmas carol, at the age of six. He had continued to turn them out throughout his life until a quarrel with his publisher put an end to them for a while. Caroline had cursed the man for damming up Strauss's genius until it occurred to her that, perhaps, these four sublime songs from the very end of his life were the distillation of his lyrical ideas from that fallow period.

She enjoyed the first two as she attended to the domestic disarray she had abandoned when she left to go on duty that morning. The third song, her favourite, transfixed her, demanding the whole of her attention. She supposed the German title would translate roughly as 'Going to Sleep', but this song was no lullaby. It began so quietly you

129

weren't sure it was there. The restrained soprano voice and the orchestra wooed each other, floating the melody across from the singer to the first violin and languidly back again. She stood immobile, unaware of her physical self and the room around her until the closing bar. In the silence that followed, the song released its hold and she resumed the tidying of Cavill's papers as she listened to the rest in a more detached way.

During her musical training, she had sometimes imagined that she would marry another musician. Then, by one of life's many ironies, she had married a musician anyway. She smiled, remembering her excitement when, as an inexperienced but promising PC, she had been co-opted on to her first murder enquiry. In the course of it, she had met Cavill who had been, at the time, the team's primary suspect.

She shook her head to clear it. To say the songs had soothed her would be to miss their point, but, having given herself over to them, she felt relaxed and refreshed. Now she was ready to make her own music. She went over to the piano and was still playing when the telephone rang. She listened to Mitchell's terse appeal and accepted his invitation to report to HQ. Deciding that she had better not interrupt his senior citizens' orchestra practice with a phone call, she left a note on the table for Cavill and departed.

Arriving at Mitchell's office, Caroline discovered that Jennifer too had been called in at this unsociable hour. Mitchell indicated armchairs, pulling one up for himself. His manner was ingratiating and Caroline suspected that his chief motive in calling them together before he had any specific instructions was to use them as a sounding board for his thoughts as he fulfilled his waiting brief. This was not an aspect of her DCI she had noticed before. She turned to Jennifer. 'What did you get from Donna Felling's school?'

Jennifer's face showed her disappointment at the

130

small amount of information her efforts had produced. Having already reported to Mitchell, she summarized her evening as briefly as possible for her colleague, adding, 'I was impressed with Miss Vardy. I went to see the child who was supposed to be Donna's friend but she couldn't say anything helpful. Her mother, though, is a JP and a friend of Diane Bates. She mentioned another child and I went along to her. I thought it might be rather late to interview a thirteen-year-old but there was no mother in to disapprove.'

'You didn't . . .?'

Jennifer shook her head. 'I didn't even go inside the house. I just asked if Donna had been in touch with her. There was a fractional pause before she shook her head. I think it would pay to go again when her mother's there.'

Mitchell nodded. 'I've spent a lot of the evening reading the child's diary. We might be right about the Bateses being a bit strapped. There's an entry about Donna overhearing a ding-dong battle between Diane and Barry.' He read from where his finger pointed. '"You're trying to compete with the Grants and it won't do. You can't recreate their interiors in our house. It doesn't work. In any case, we aren't in their class financially . . ."'

Jennifer smiled. 'She's got an excellent verbal memory.' Looking over Mitchell's shoulder, she scanned the passage for herself. 'She can spell it all too.'

Mitchell grinned. 'I'll take your word for that. There's a long entry about four months ago. Her mother had spoiled her birthday party and upset some of her friends and Donna was furious. She threatened – in writing – to kill her.'

Caroline was sufficiently shocked to interrupt. 'You aren't seriously considering Donna?'

'Why not?'

Caroline paused to analyse her revulsion at the idea. 'Well, even if struggling made Lorraine's death quick – even if she had a physical idiosyncrasy that made her specially vulnerable – it would have taken two to three

131

minutes, according to Dr Holland, for her to die. That would be an eternity to a thirteen-year-old. It would mean a very deliberate intention. In spite of the desperation of her situation, I think the girl genuinely loved her mother. In any case, if she was so incensed by a spoiled party, why would she wait four months?'

'Not because of the birthday. But, what if she was equally angry about the funeral? By all accounts she was very fond of her grandfather. But, no, I wasn't seriously considering Donna, although it's got to remain a possibility. A bit later on there's another passage about how her mother's men friends "try it on" with her.'

'Did they?'

'I can't tell you. I've sent Elinor round to see what Diane thinks.' Mitchell turned back to Jennifer. 'Maybe your sensible Miss Vardy might know, or at least make an intelligent guess, though I suppose she'd have mentioned it already if she had any such suspicions.'

'But, if even one of them had . . .'

'Precisely. Where might that one be now and is Donna with him?'

Caroline interrupted again. 'And, if it isn't true, there's still the question of what Nicholas Felling would do if he believed it was.'

Caroline stifled a yawn and willed Mitchell, who drank coffee constantly, to produce some now. Not picking up this signal, Mitchell merely continued, 'Talking of Felling, I had a last look round his house today. I think we should let him have it back as soon as possible. He'll need it when he gets Donna back –'

'If he gets Donna back.'

Mitchell ignored the interruption. 'It reminded me how much he'd given up in terms of comfort and space. Some of his books are still there. It could be that he has no room for any more at Victoria Road or it might have been that needing one of them provided him with an excuse to visit more often.'

'If Lorraine's left almost everything to him he'll be

able to move straight back in. I wonder if he knew about the will?'

Mitchell shrugged and consulted his notes. 'What else haven't I told you? . . . Our friend John Kennedy has been arrested and charged with burglary, just the one at Elm Road to begin with but he's asked for nineteen other offences to be taken into consideration.'

'And what about our friend Craig Potter who was paying his blackmail money to Mr Scott?'

Mitchell frowned. 'I'm not sure. He's saying nothing and we've banged him up to have a think about things. I wondered at first if the reason for their meetings could be private and quite trivial.'

'Sex, you mean?'

'I even wondered if it could be just a hobby. I had an uncle who was a chess fanatic. He not only played with a partner across the board like normal people but he had scores of games going with people he only saw occasionally. They'd send their moves to each other by post and a game could take weeks.'

'But Potter's let us put him in a cell rather than explain.'

'Quite. Maybe Scott was stealing drugs from the hospital and selling them. He'd have a lot to lose though. You and I had better have a joint assault on young Craig in the morning. He might have changed his tune after a night away from his lady friend, especially if he's been without some noxious substance he's used to getting from Scott. I'll give the station a ring and get a medic to have a look at him to be on the safe side.'

Caroline, now in serious danger of falling asleep in her chair, suddenly roused herself and wondered which suspect or member of the team was in need of a doctor. She was profoundly grateful when the exchange between her two senior officers was interrupted by Mitchell's telephone. He listened carefully to his caller before assuring him, 'They're on their way.' He passed on the brief explanation, 'There's a Debbie and Mrs Collins downstairs. Is that the girl you were talking about?' Jennifer nodded.

'Donna's been with them but she's gone again.' The two women hurried away.

They arrived in the station foyer to find that a WPC had taken their visitors to the canteen. Cheered, they went down to find it comfortingly warm and more or less empty. Both officers were pleased. They had interviewed children and their anxious parents there before if it was quiet enough. There was an unofficial atmosphere and to have interviewees eating and drinking put them off their guard.

Opposite the WPC sat a heavily made-up but skimpily dressed woman whose cleavage and knees were sufficiently well preserved for their revelation to be not repulsive. Beside the woman sat a cheerful-looking teenaged girl in a garish anorak. The girl was wiping her greasy fingers with a paper napkin which she dropped on top of the pile of crumbs on her plate. In front of the mother was a hardly-touched iced cake. The WPC urged her to eat it but Mrs Collins shook her head with a small shudder and a complacent pat of her flat midriff.

Her daughter eyed the cake longingly. The girl was already considerably overweight, her breasts full and pendulous and her stomach a rounded hummock below her fleshy midriff. Yet, she had a raffish attraction. Her hair was thick and dark and her colour high and vivid. The eyes sparkled and challenged, but her manner was not confrontational. She was unfazed by her surroundings. She had come to give them information and she would do it in a straightforward way.

Caroline indicated the mother's plate. 'You don't want that?' Mrs Collins shook her head. 'Can I have it then? I'm starving.' Ignoring Debbie's indignant glance, Caroline consumed the confection in two bites before settling into a chair. 'Don't worry about my waistline,' she assured the visitors. 'This job keeps me on the run. I'll chase a few villains in the morning and this won't show.'

A glare from Jennifer told her she was wasting time. She didn't agree. Time spent establishing the right atmosphere was always time well spent. The mother might have been offended but the girl, momentarily distracted from her anxiety, was laughing. 'Blimey! I've seen you before. You're that copper that Jonno can beat?'

'That's one of my colleagues. If Jonno is your twelve-earringed friend with the purple tuft, then he can certainly run well but he owes his prizes to DC Clement for the good training he's been given. I hear you've got something to tell me about another friend.'

Debbie cast an agonized glance at her mother, then seemed to decide that whatever she feared from her was less important than her responsibilities to her friend. 'I was bunking off today.'

'Off school?'

'Right. And Donna rang me on the off-chance.'

'That you'd be at home and would help her?'

'Right. She was upset because her dad had dumped her on that snooty cow she's been staying with. Said she wasn't going there.'

'Where was she ringing from?'

'She didn't say but she arrived in only a few minutes. We sat drinking Coke and trying to think what to do but we couldn't come up with anything very good. I said she could hide in my bedroom when Mum came home from work.'

'So, Donna was intending to stay the night with you?'

Debbie nodded. 'But she's a bit fussy. She wouldn't wear any of my underclothes, or sleep in what she'd had on all day – and she definitely wouldn't have put on the same knickers tomorrow. She said she'd ring for some more stuff, but by the time she'd thought of it, Mum was due back.'

'So she went to phone from somewhere else?'

'Right.'

'And how was she going to get back in?'

'It was well after school. She could call round for me, just ordinary like. Then she could stay till Mum went out. Then I'd get her some tea and we could watch telly till it was time to hide again when Mum and Jim came back.'

'But Donna didn't come back.'

135

Debbie bit her lip and nodded. 'I panicked.'

'Didn't you think she'd just met someone, that she'd be along a bit later?'

Debbie gave Caroline a pitying look. 'In the dark? Not Donna! She wasn't very . . .'

'Streetwise?'

'Right.'

'Or, wasn't it likely that whoever had been asked for the clothes had insisted on taking her home? Who was it, anyway?'

Debbie shrugged at the second question and answered the first. 'She'd have let me know. She has good manners. Anyway, I rang the police station without giving my name and asked if she was still missing. They started on a load of questions so I hung up. Not before Mum had listened in, though, and she carried on till she got the whole story. Now she's furious because she's had to leave Jim and come here.'

Caroline wondered why the mother was so silent during this exchange. Because she had the wisdom to let her daughter finish an admirably clear account? She thought not. More likely the fury of which Debbie accused her. But not, Caroline decided, a lack of concern. The body language between mother and daughter showed a contented acceptance of one another, in spite of surface disapproval. Something like what Donna had shared with Lorraine.

Eventually, Jennifer escorted mother and daughter to the foyer where she arranged for a car to take them home. Caroline, waiting there for her to return, wondered what her next orders would be. She was now fully alert, which was fortunate. As her sergeant came back in and they turned towards the lift, the desk sergeant, wordier than Magic, called out to them. 'Ladies, there's a message for you. There's been a hit and run, a couple of hours ago. It was just beyond the end of the precinct at Birkbourne, outside the RSPCA. A young girl in intensive care at the Royal.'

Wordlessly, they turned round and left the building.

*   *   *

Clement entered the station foyer satisfied that his action sheet was completed, but dissatisfied with every other aspect of his life. He had hoped to accompany Mitchell to the hospital and had been disgruntled to learn that he had been passed over in favour, not of his sergeant but of Shakila. It was not fair. He had done his best to help the girl worm her way into Cloughton's CID and now it looked as though she might humiliate him by being made up to sergeant first. Mitchell's call had been brief. 'Shakila's on the spot.' Wasn't she always? 'The most useful thing you can do is sleep. You're off duty from now for four hours. After that it's my turn and you and Caroline will be answerable to Jennifer until I reappear.'

Clement was annoyed. By then everything would be sorted out with just the clearing up to do. Still, that would include hunting a murderer, even, possibly, two of them. In any case, he was not brave enough to argue with Mitchell about something so trivial – and he had his pride!

He never found it easy to sleep to order, especially when he was on an adrenaline high. His usual insomnia cure had two parts, a hard run and a huge mug of cocoa. Since Mitchell had allowed him only four hours, he cut his usual circuitous route home by half. Sweating copiously, he slowed for the warm-down half-mile and recognized the youth watching him from the shelter of the betting shop doorway.

The youth looked less than pleased to see him. 'Going home for your bedtime cocoa?'

Clement slowed to a stop and scowled with mock annoyance. 'Jonno been giving away my winning secrets? He's going to regret it. Anyway, it's alcoholic cocoa.' He wiped the sweat out of his eyes. 'How's life treating you then, Shaun? Got a tip to share?'

Shaun was not impressed by the change to a friendlier tone. 'Never mind the chat-up. You only talk to me to nick me or when you think I can tell you something you're too dumb to work out yourself.'

Clement nodded his agreement. 'Got it in two. We've a mutual friend – called Debbie.'

'Well, she won't have grassed me up, so I'm only in danger from you. I think I'll sleep tonight.'

Clement dropped down to sit alongside the boy on the shop's doorstep. 'Debbie Collins a grasser? Course she isn't. Your name just came up in the course of our interesting conversation.' He reached into the bum bag buckled round his waist, took out a block of chocolate and offered half of it to Shaun. They chewed companionably for some moments.

'Go on then. What do I know that you need to know?'

'Such co-operation all of a sudden.'

'Maybe I want something that you've got.'

Clement was suspicious. 'Like what?'

The boy said, with some embarrassment, 'If a fool like Jonno can win a few hundred quid just jogging along a sheep track, how about you taking a real athlete on?'

Clement was speechless, half with astonishment, half with delight. Keeping his face deadpan he regarded the young thug for some seconds before opening negotiations. 'That hit and run.'

'What about it?'

'All about it. What can you tell me?'

Shaun scratched his head in tantalizing parody of searching his memory before he shrugged. 'Not a lot.' He enjoyed watching Clement's face fall before going on. 'But if you mean that one Jonno says he saw outside the RSPCA, I could release him from my threat to mash up his face if he goes running to you lot about it.'

Careful not to show too much gratitude, Clement raised a hand in salute to his new ally and walked away.

Chapter Nine

If either Mitchell or Jennifer had worked out any clever psychological tricks to persuade Craig Potter to reveal all he knew they had wasted their time. On Friday morning, as they walked into the interview room where he awaited them, the boy pushed back his chair from the scratched table. He had obviously not slept. There were dark rings under his eyes, though his skin was young and supple enough to have remained uncrumpled. His shaved head was covered with light brown stubble which matched that on his chin and cheeks.

He met Jennifer's eye, then dropped his gaze to the table as he muttered, 'OK, you were right. It's drugs. But it's not like you think.' It was, indeed, not the story they were expecting. Of course he was not on coke or crack, he insisted indignantly. He had more sense. 'This was different, though. I did it for the money but I did it to help other people as well. After all, someone had to be the first to try it and it was better for it to be someone young and healthy like me. I could cope with the side effects better than somebody who was already ill and weak.'

Putting her hand on Craig's shoulder, Jennifer pushed him gently back on to his chair. She pulled up another and sat beside him. 'I think I understand what you're telling me, Craig. Can you just wait until Chief Inspector Mitchell has switched on the tape recorder?'

Mitchell hastily carried out the implied instruction, dictating the names of the people present, the date and the time. He smiled encouragingly at the boy. 'Mr Potter has just told us that he is being paid by Mr Neville Scott to be a guinea pig for drugs he has developed as a treatment for Addison's disease.'

Craig nodded, thankful to have the words found for him and to have the worrying situation out in the open. He spoke slowly and loudly to the machine, as the British do to foreigners. 'I agree with what Chief Inspector Mitchell has just said.' As the conversation went on he became accustomed to the situation and forgot the recording.

He was strong in Scott's defence. 'He wouldn't let my health suffer. He promised. I had a full medical examination every month.'

'Where was this, Craig?'

'Usually it was at his house. He didn't want to get into trouble from the hospital people, you see. Every so often, we risked going to the hospital because he wanted to use equipment he hadn't got at home.' Mitchell and Jennifer exchanged worried looks.

'Can you describe these examinations?'

Craig did so, in detail and without the slightest embarrassment, convincing both officers that at least the examinations had not been a cloak for any kind of assault. The boy explained in detail how the scheme had worked. Meetings had taken place in various pubs, never the same one twice. Money and a supply of the pills were exchanged for written replies to a list of questions about his physical reactions to his 'treatment'.

Yes, he did have a job. It was with an insurance company. 'But I'm not earning much because I'm still being trained. I needed money to take Brenda out and about like she was used to. She's been paying for most things but she's bound to get fed up with that. Anyway, you have your pride, don't you?'

'Wouldn't you rather have your health?'

'But, I told you . . .'

Mitchell sighed and reluctantly gave him permission to leave and return to his lady friend. The situation as it related to Scott he could deal with. The boy he could only pray for.

*   *   *

Caroline was pleased to be driving to Manchester even though there was a sheet of water on the M62 and her windscreen wipers were trying to hypnotize her. She wasn't sure how talking to Toni Grant would help their enquiry but she had wanted the chance to see the members of this odd family through the eyes of someone who knew them well but was not yet quite one of them.

Until she displayed her warrant card, the hotel receptionist had been unwilling to rouse its guest. At first, Toni herself had been annoyed at being disturbed so early in the morning. Once she was told, however, that her future sister-in-law was critically injured she was anxious to give all the help she could, including ordering breakfast for the two of them to be sent up to her room.

Caroline tried to work out whether or not Toni Grant was good-looking. She decided not, though everything had been done that money could do to improve the woman's appearance. The hair was beautifully cut to flatter a rather thin face with small eyes and a sharp nose. Toni had a good firm chin, however, that prevented her expression from being peevish. People would notice the elegant clothes rather than the woman inside them.

She chattered on fashion topics to set Miss Grant at her ease and off her guard and both women were munching buttered crumpets before Caroline asked, 'Can you tell me when was the last time that you actually saw Donna?'

Toni stopped chewing and thought hard. 'I don't think I've seen her since Phil and I went round to the Granby Arms on Wednesday morning and I hardly spoke to her then. She was drugged up to the eyes and, in any case, she was in no mood for a chat after what had happened, poor kid.'

'We've been given to understand that you two didn't get on well together.'

'Well, no. We've hardly had the chance to really. I'm old enough to be classed as one of the grown-ups who all disapprove of her. She knows that I really did disapprove of her mother and she resented that. Worse than all that, as she sees things, I'm stealing away her beloved brother. I'm afraid I'm the last person she would run to or trust.'

'Can you suggest someone she does trust?'

'She doesn't have a lot of opportunity to make friends. She never mixed freely with other girls out of school because she felt responsible for her mother. She had a good friend called Helen who moved away. Now there's an odious child called Rachel something or other, thrust at her by Diane because her mother's a JP. Still, what can you expect in the way of discrimination in any field of a woman whose windows are dressed like Dresden shepherdesses and whose bathroom carpet is pink? But Donna does have one real friend who's a gem. Vulgar and brash and proud of it. She has the same sort of insecure background as Donna but it's made her tough, self-reliant and loyal.'

'So, Donna trusts you sufficiently to talk about her friends to you.'

'No, I got to know Debbie when she presented herself at the house one day last year and asked to see me. She said she needed to earn some money and Donna had told her we had horses. Could she muck them out for me.'

'You took her on?'

'After I'd spent weeks teaching her. She'd never come face to face with a horse in her life before but she learned quickly and works hard. Donna will be all right if she's run to Debbie, bless her black-ringed little eyes. Have you tried there?'

'She and her mother came to the station, to say Donna did go to them first. She went out some time around five to make a telephone call and never came back.'

'My God! Who was it to? What did she say?'

For the moment, Caroline made no comment on this strange reply. 'We were hoping that someone, perhaps you, could make a good guess.'

Toni wiped her buttery lips. 'Her father's the obvious choice.'

'But she ran away in the first place because there was a misunderstanding. She thought he'd gone back on his promise to have her living with him and arranged for her to live with her aunt and uncle.'

'Misunderstanding?' Toni's tone was scornful. 'More like mischief-making on her aunt's part if you ask me. Try Philip, then.'

'He was out.'

She put her hand to her head. 'So he was. I called in yesterday afternoon to collect the shoes I'm wearing. I suppose, by the way, that you'll have to complete your questioning by asking where I was at the relevant time.' Caroline nodded gratefully. 'Right. Where do I start?'

'Just after lunch.'

'I had that with my PA, sorting out my diary for the next few days. Then I went back to my flat. It's at the top of my parents' house, convenient for all sorts of reasons. I discovered my shoes were at Phil's so I popped round, picked them up, made myself a coffee and then came across here before the rush hour and before the rain started, thank goodness. I had a cup of tea with Zelda. The show started at seven thirty and I sat with her brother Patrick. Zelda went on to a party with some theatre people and Patrick and I had a drink. He dropped me here just minutes before you arrived.'

She flushed an ugly red as she realized how much this casual remark had revealed. She reached for a piece of hotel notepaper, scribbled the man's name and telephone number on it and held it out.

Caroline noted down the main points from Toni's account. 'I don't suppose we'll need it but thanks anyway.' She was disappointed. Her interview seemed to have been unproductive, certainly not worth a double drive across the Pennines. At least she was thankful that the rain had stopped at last.

Mitchell had wondered if he should hold their next discussion with Felling himself, but decided eventually that it needed a woman's touch. Jennifer, therefore, having negotiated with a nurse at the door of the IC ward at the Royal

Hospital, went in to find Felling sitting at his daughter's bedside, holding her hand. A triangle in the middle of Donna's face seemed to be the only part of her that was not covered by dressings and bandages. Within the triangle, tubes went into or came out of every orifice.

Jennifer crept across to the bed and put a hand on Felling's shoulder. 'How is she?' she whispered.

Felling made no reply and the two adults stood and watched the girl, both lost in their own thoughts. After a while Felling half turned his head. 'I've never done anything before that you could classify as a crime but I'm going to kill for this. First whoever did it and then Diane for causing it to happen.'

Jennifer ignored the threat. 'Help us to find him then.'

He turned a tear-streaked face towards her. 'She's got a fifty-fifty chance, they say – and if she lives they don't know what sort of life it will be.'

The sister came over with an appeal to Jennifer. 'Take him down to the canteen and make him have something to eat.' She turned to the frantic father. 'I've told you already, Mr Felling, but I'll tell you again. Donna's under sedation. There's no chance of her waking up and asking for you in the next hour. What will happen unless you're more sensible is that, when she does become aware that you're here and wants you, you'll have collapsed and then you'll be of no earthly use to her.'

He was not convinced. 'You can't be sure. What if she should wake, against all odds? Or what if she suddenly gets worse?'

The sister considered. 'Well, there's a loudspeaker system reaching all over the building. To be perfectly honest, it is difficult to hear if the canteen happens to be noisy. Have you got a mobile phone?'

Felling shook his head.

'I have,' put in Jennifer, fishing it out of her pocket and offering it. She earned a grateful smile from the sister as she scribbled the number and handed over the scrap of paper. The kindly woman stowed it away under her overall and warned Jennifer not to switch on her phone until she was actually in the canteen.

Eventually Felling was persuaded. 'Just long enough for something to eat then.'

Ten minutes later, he and Jennifer sat opposite each other, two mixed grills on plates between them. After a moment's hesitation, Felling tucked in, half guiltily. 'It seems heartless, but actually I am very hungry.'

'You don't have to apologize for it.'

For some minutes they ate in silence, Jennifer fastidiously heaping cut-off portions of fatty meat round the edge of her plate, and giving the hospital canteen a poor second place to that enjoyed by the police.

His plate clean, Felling laid down his knife and fork and looked at his watch before pulling his cooling coffee towards him.

'You've only been away twenty minutes. Feeling better?'

'Yes thanks. Now I must –'

'An hour the sister said and I'm afraid I need to talk to you for some of it.'

'About Donna?'

Jennifer shook her head. 'No, about who killed Lorraine. Shall we walk in the conservatory for a few minutes? You could do with some fresh air but it's a bit too dark and cold outside to be pleasant – and the phone has to be off in the main building.'

He nodded and followed her out into the enclosed raised-bed garden. Jennifer stopped to read a plaque telling her that the huge glass construction was the gift of the hospital charity fund. She supposed that it had consoled a good many worried relatives before him. She observed that the beds were less meticulously cared for than the last time she had had occasion to pass through. Nevertheless it was an attractive and cheerful setting with its masses of early winter pansies and some dishevelled miniature dahlias, quite out of keeping with the content of their conversation.

They had come to a halt by a bench donated in memory

145

of a venerable council member and now they sat, one at either end of it.

'Because I want you to be back in the ward well within your hour,' Jennifer told Felling, 'I'm going in for the kill.' Felling nodded his appreciation. 'We have our list of suspects, though we realize that the name of Lorraine's killer may not yet be on it. However, you, like almost all the people who attended Mr Smith's funeral, are fairly high on it. This is how we see it. You've given up a good house and a good slice of your income, only to watch your former partner drink it away, making your daughter's life very difficult in the process. In addition, if her diary is to be believed, she was in moral danger from some of her mother's later partners –'

'What!' Felling had sprung to his feet, his fists clenched. 'What the hell are you talking about?'

'To be honest,' Jennifer admitted, 'I'm not sure. I might be talking about an imaginative little girl weaving fairy stories. However, I might be talking about the same little girl, damaged in yet another way by the men your ex-partner preferred to you.'

Slowly Felling sank down again on to the bench. 'Is there anything else you haven't told me?' His body was shaking but his voice was steady.

'Not that I know about.'

'So, at worst Donna has been assaulted and at best, her idea of fun is to fantasize that she has. I never imagined that Lorraine –'

'I think that what you imagined was the truth.' Jennifer was not sure whether he was hearing her. He stared with a blank face at the innocent row of dahlias. She stood up and spoke briskly. 'Just let us know if you think of anything that might help to eliminate you. Shall we walk back?'

He rose and followed her back inside, pausing at the door. 'You did have Donna's word that I didn't go upstairs.'

'That's not valid evidence in the circumstances. Keep

thinking over everything you saw. I hope to hear from you soon, especially if it's good news of Donna.'

As she climbed into her car, Jennifer thought about Felling's threat to kill the man who had injured his daughter. It would come more easily to a man who had killed once already.

Later that day it was Clement's turn to drive to Manchester. His journey was pleasanter than Caroline's had been, in broad daylight on a dry road, though the bright autumn sun had dazzled him for some of the way.

He was in good time for the arrival of Neville Scott's flight, which, anyway, was certain to be late. He was looking forward, therefore, to prowling and plane-spotting for a while like the overgrown schoolboy he knew he was.

Scott frustrated him by arriving twenty minutes early. He had returned from the Saudi trip unrepentant. 'My patient needed the operation. I'd already given you such information as was likely to help you. All the travelling arrangements were made and I wanted the fee. The best way to convince you that I wasn't fleeing from justice was to go and then return as planned.'

Since he had done just that, it seemed a waste of time to prolong the argument. Instead, Clement informed the recalcitrant consultant, 'We know now what you wanted the fee for. Do you realize that you've ruined your career?'

He was glad when Scott shrugged rather than challenged him. 'I haven't harmed any of the lads.'

Clement gaped at him. 'How the hell many are there?'

Scott treated the question as rhetorical and suggested that they should collect his luggage from the carousel. The extortion of answers could come later, Clement decided. First he'd take what was being offered willingly.

He would try an exchange of information. 'We got what we know from Craig Potter.'

Scott's face registered genuine disappointment. 'So Lorraine did give my game away.'

Clement explained what Lorraine had thought she was investigating, and Scott, impressed by Lorraine's practical use of her dramatic talent, remained urbane and chatty. 'I did rather want to get her on her own and explain. I didn't think it would be a problem. Lorraine would have understood. She went her own way too, got what she wanted by unorthodox methods if they worked better. Hell! There's nothing physically wrong with young Potter, is there?'

'There doesn't appear to be. I'm sure he'll appreciate your concern when I tell him.'

Scott glared. 'I don't expect you to approve but please don't make a joke of it. Have you ever seen a person suffering from Addison's disease?'

Humbly, Clement shook his head and allowed Scott to drive home from Manchester in his own vehicle.

Chapter Ten

On Saturday morning, Mitchell and Jennifer were sitting dispiritedly, one each side of his desk. The time was seven fifteen and they had already spent a quarter of an hour leafing through one after another of the documents in the case file. Each encouraged the other with remarks that neither of them believed. 'The answer is bound to be in here somewhere.' 'It's just a matter of looking at it all with fresh eyes.'

Their eyes, no longer fresh, were still looking to no avail by the time the team reported in an hour later. Mitchell called for everyone's attention and went through the motions of the briefing. The men and women in front of him looked just as he felt. He was sending them out, all over town, to continue a routine searching and questioning for which they had lost all enthusiasm. They too no longer believed their activities would produce that vital piece of evidence they needed. Even Beardsmore accepted his action sheet without a smile.

Mitchell had decided to keep behind the borrowed DCs, together with Jennifer and Caroline. They all regarded him enquiringly, even with a glimmer of interest. Did he have a plan, a fresh approach?

Mitchell laughed. 'Don't look at me as though I'm about to produce a magic solution like a rabbit out of a hat.'

David Guest looked disappointed and began to tidy away the sheets that were spread over the CI's desk. Mitchell raised a hand and shook his head to stop him. 'Leave the file out and we'll try something else. Maybe this is just kids' antics but they can't lead to a bigger blank than we've drawn up to now.'

He scrabbled in a drawer and drew out several sheets of lined file paper, giving them two each. 'I've played this game many times before. It's not a magic formula but it seldom fails to move us a bit further on. There's a name on each sheet,' he told them. 'Forget everybody else. Concentrate on making the best case you can against each of the two people I've allocated to you. You've got until this afternoon's briefing at two.'

Guest frowned as he looked up from his two sheets. 'Donna Felling? She was mown down because she was threatening to name her mother's killer?'

'So? It might seem to her a good way of diverting suspicion from herself.'

'Presumably she didn't run herself over!'

Mitchell sighed. 'David, just get on with what I've asked you to do.'

Jennifer wondered whether she too would get short shrift. Nevertheless she still asked, 'Did you put Victor Grant in just to make the numbers up, or do you seriously consider him a suspect? He was still in Hanover on Tuesday afternoon.'

'So he says.'

Jennifer nodded. 'OK. Has anybody interviewed him?'

Caroline looked up. 'Not all by himself. He answered a few questions when I met him at Conroy's flat.'

Mitchell sighed again. 'Right, Jennifer, better go and see him now. I'm afraid he's slipped through the net if there's no report of anyone seeing him on his own.'

On her way downstairs, a few minutes later, Jennifer met Shakila coming up. As usual, the young DC had completed her assignment and had come back, as she admitted frankly, 'to hang around with an eye to the main chance.'

Jennifer smiled. 'That could include helping me track down Victor Grant.'

Shakila, delighted, asked, 'Do we want him for anything in particular?'

'Because, in the CI's words, he's slipped through the net.'

Shakila was puzzled. 'He wasn't in the country. We've checked with the airline.'

'Only by phone. We're usually more thorough.'

'OK.' Shakila turned to follow her sergeant back down the stairs and out to the car park. 'His house, then?'

Jennifer shook her head. 'Tried ringing. Then I tried his firm on the off-chance and got Philip Conroy.'

'On Saturday?'

'Grant making up for his time abroad and Conroy drowning his sorrows in work, maybe. He said some of the staff work regularly on a Saturday morning, several in the office and a few in the garage, checking over the firm's vehicles ready for Monday. Grant's out with clients all day and not due back in the office till Monday.'

'Any named?'

'Said he doesn't know.'

Shakila's tone was world-weary. 'He would, I suppose, especially if his boss isn't with clients.'

Jennifer hid a grin. 'Have we any reason to think that?'

'He's got that look.'

'He's also got that reputation. His wife, then?' They nodded sagely at each other and climbed into Jennifer's car.

As the sergeant drove, Shakila telephoned again. This time Glenda Grant answered. She would make time to speak with them but her husband was golfing, 'half business, half pleasure'. Grinning to herself, Shakila reached for the road atlas in the passenger door and checked their route to the village just four miles south of Cloughton, where the Grants' house, much photographed by the local press, lay.

They found it with no difficulty as it seemed to be the focal point around which the rest of the place had been built. Double-fronted, in mellow pink brick, it was very attractive. They knew, from various fulsome *Clarion* articles, that it had begun its existence as an early nineteenth-century, two-bedroomed cottage which had been continually extended. The additions looked interesting rather than piecemeal.

The house and garden were protected by a tall beech hedge. A gravelled drive led off the village street to a parking area in front of the house, then continued through tall timber gates, presumably to a garage. Leaving the car, they paused to admire a York stone terrace. 'These people at least don't seem hard up,' Jennifer remarked. Seeing no bell or knocker, she rapped on a panel of the dark green painted door.

The door was opened by a girl whose manner suggested that she was a maid, though she wore no uniform. She might be an au pair or a housekeeper. A woman stood behind the girl, giving personal attention to her visitors but leaving her employee to fuss with the door and hang the officers' jackets.

They stood, on a thick but plain wool carpet, in a vast hall furnished with two huge leather sofas and a hall stand and bookcase in dark wood. A functional roller blind at a tall window was softened by heavy curtains at each side. The only decoration was provided by a bowl of shaggy dahlias on a small table. Glenda Grant moved the flowers to the window sill, giving instructions over her shoulder. 'We'll have coffee out here, Marie.'

So, Shakila noted, no attempt to display the rest of the splendours. She watched Mrs Grant take out a tissue to mop up a drip of water from the vase, then turned to hiss to Jennifer, 'Old money. Hers, I'd bet.' Jennifer nodded, half an acknowledgement, half a warning to keep personal comments until later. Shakila subsided and made only silent observations.

Glenda Grant's hair was a beautifully cut cap, but fine and thin, and an undyed mixture of fair and grey. The features were delicate so that the large nose jarred. The brows were plucked but Shakila suspected it had been done to tidy up rather than to beautify the face. The black skirt and grey sweater were the same clothes that had been worn at the funeral on Tuesday and small stud earrings were the only jewellery.

Shakila noted with interest the bitten nails but their interviewee showed no other sign of being ill at ease. She seemed a woman of few words, but not unfriendly, making a nice distinction between her manner to the girl and to themselves. Shakila settled to enjoy the battle of words between her sergeant and their victim.

Mrs Grant took the initiative. 'I'm not sure why you've come. There's very little I can add to what I told you on Tuesday night.'

'Remind me.'

'I can't believe in inefficiency from someone of your rank and bearing.'

'All right, you said you were representing your daughter who is about to marry the grandson of the deceased Mr Edgar Smith. That was the only fact you offered – so little that we thought there must be more.'

'I said I was barely acquainted with the deceased Mrs Conroy.'

'True.'

There was a silence which Jennifer hoped Mrs Grant would fill. All it produced was an exasperated expression. After some moments, Mrs Grant requested, with some asperity, 'Please ask me what you want to know. I'll willingly put off my morning's business to help with your investigation, but not to play verbal games with you!'

This evidently persuaded Jennifer that the interview would be better conducted by her DC's blunt methods. Shakila was delighted to receive the nod that permitted her to take over. Quickly, she considered her options. Caroline had described this woman as diffident. Maybe she felt more confident on home ground.

She grinned at Mrs Grant. 'To find out what we really want to know, our questions would be rather out of order, especially in your social circle.'

This caused some amusement. 'Try me.'

Shakila accepted the challenge. 'How did – or, do – you feel about the family your daughter is marrying into? In particular, about the dead woman who would have been her mother-in-law? And, if that doesn't get us thrown out, the other question is, why didn't your daughter, even if not your husband, make herself free to attend the funeral of a member of her fiancé's close family?'

Mrs Grant nodded. 'Hm. I see your dilemma. Your questions are blunt and personal, but not in the circumstances impertinent. I was present because I was brought up to fulfil my social obligations. Victor wasn't, and doesn't put pressure on our daughter to do so. Toni did attend the actual service.

'I don't see how it helps your case, but, to answer your first question, I found Mrs Conroy refreshing, though I think we'd have had nothing in common. I find Mrs Bates a rather silly woman, but I'm sure Toni would have had no problem dealing with her.'

Shakila glanced at Jennifer for permission to take further liberties. Jennifer's head didn't move. So, at least it wasn't a shake. Forge ahead then.

Glenda Grant watched this interplay with interest. Shakila tried to decide how much more leeway she had with both her companions, then took the plunge. 'Perhaps your tolerance of Mrs Conroy's behaviour in some respects is because there are members of your own family who are open to criticism.' Both officers waited in some trepidation.

Mrs Grant replied calmly. 'You mean Victor's various liaisons, I suppose. I'm answering you honestly because I envy you.' Jennifer waited for an explanation, which was not forthcoming. Shakila knew that the woman coveted her own free spirit that would neither accept unjustified humiliation nor fear to take risks.

'I'm aware that his golfing partner – if he is actually playing as he said he intended – is very likely female. I know too that some of his business discussions are conducted in bed. Unlike you, I've been prepared to tolerate the situation, assuring myself that they're all at least respectable. I could convince the more gullible of my friends that these "business meetings" were necessary,

even that he'd prefer me to be helping with the entertainment if I didn't find it unutterably boring. He's on his
last chance now, though and he knows it.'

'You'd leave him?'

'Good heavens, no. We couldn't have capers like that in
this family.'

'So, you'd . . .?'

'Pull my fifty-one per cent of shares out of what he has
the cheek to call his business.'

After Jennifer's departure, a brooding silence had fallen in
Mitchell's office, which, but for sighs, whispered mutter-
ings and the shuffling of papers, went on for three-quarters
of an hour. Then, Mitchell's pet civilian typist brought
them more of her special brew of coffee and cream.

The atmosphere lightened a little but most of the assembled officers continued working as they drank it. After
another half-hour Mitchell relented and spoke to the tops
of Guest's and Cranton's heads. 'Since neither of you has
made an excuse to sneak off for a smoke you can have an
official one now. I know your brains run on nicotine and
I wouldn't like the case to founder because you'd run out
of fuel.'

The two men left speedily, glad, in Clement's absence, to
escape a diatribe on the evils of smoking and the benefits
of fresh air and exercise.

Mitchell and Caroline remained at the desk. Seconds
passed that seemed like hours. Then Mitchell became
aware, from his DC's sudden stillness, that she had picked
up some point she had not noticed before. He asked no
questions, knowing how easily an ephemeral idea could be
lost. Caroline went on studying the piece of paper in her
hand. Then she reached for a pen and made jottings in the
margin. Now it was safer to ask. The idea, whatever it was,
had been caught in writing. 'What have you got there?'

'The report on the first session with Philip Conroy.'

'What about it?'

'Nothing in itself. Can you see the report I wrote on my session with Antonia Grant in Manchester?'

Mitchell sifted through the heaped documents and handed her the required sheet. She read it through carefully, underlining a couple of sentences. Startled, she looked up. 'I thought that was what I remembered. Everyone has been telling us Toni Grant went straight on to her business meeting after the church service on Tuesday but when we saw Grant the other day, in Philip Conroy's flat, he referred to lunch with an Australian wool merchant.'

'Slip of the tongue?'

'Philip said he was away himself on Monday and it was Toni who picked up Diane's doorkey. She had it for a chunk of Monday, plenty of time to get a duplicate made.'

'Right.'

'And – another thing – when she bounced in whilst I was talking to Philip at his flat she said she'd never been inside Diane's house apart from standing in the hall doorway for a few minutes on Monday. Then the next thing we know she's telling me all about the tastelessness of her window dressings.'

'Maybe she could see how awful they were from the outside.'

'But not the pink bathroom carpet.'

'Maybe Philip told her about it.'

'You're having to try very hard.'

'OK. Can you check what she drives?'

'I've already done that. She's got a blue Megane of her own and a white Merc as a company car.'

'And Jonathan Stepney was quite sure that the car that hit Donna was a grey Escort? He must have been at least thirty yards away.'

'I'd back him on cars, except maybe the colour under street lamps. He wouldn't get confused between a small Ford and a white Merc.'

'And we've not come across anyone concerned with the case who drives an Escort?' Caroline shook her head dolefully. 'Oh well, we knew we'd have to bear in mind the possibility of two killers.'

Mitchell reached again for the three documents that justified his DC's present suspicions. 'I wonder if, when Donna said she'd seen her brother and Toni Grant in a clinch on the landing at her aunt's house, she might have been telling the truth.'

'Not necessarily. Philip could have been in on the whole plan but it could have been done without his knowing. Antonia could have gone straight to Elm Road from the church and hidden herself before Philip arrived.'

'But Donna . . .'

'Seeing Antonia on the landing when she wasn't supposed to be there might have triggered off another of her fantasies. What I really don't understand is what motive she could have had. She didn't need the money they thought Philip was going to get. By her standards it wasn't much anyway.'

Mitchell smiled. 'Rich people never think they've got enough money. Perhaps it was just that Toni wasn't prepared to put up with the social embarrassment of having a drunkard for a mother-in-law. According to Grant, she had continually put off the wedding date until suddenly, this week, they decided to name the day – after the embarrassment had been removed. Grant was celebrating with Philip, though, strangely, not with Antonia, and they were well down a 1976 Nuits-St-Georges.'

'And the scratches on her face – they were where Lorraine struggled and scratched her?'

'Oh come on, Caroline. Have you never been blackberrying? Those scratches were surely made by brambles as she claimed.'

'Yes, to disguise the one deep puncture made by one of Lorraine's painted talons.'

A happy picture appeared in Mitchell's mind. 'You mean she went and rolled in . . .?' They giggled delightedly for a second at the idea of the elegant Toni rubbing her carefully preserved face in a tangle of brambles.

'Do you think there were nettles as well? I do hope so.'

157

Mitchell stopped laughing and continued to examine their theory. 'So, Lorraine's fingernails puncture Antonia's cheek and she grabs Lorraine's handkerchief from the pillow to dab blood away, probably wrinkling her aristocratic nose at the smell of it. Then she stuffs it in her pocket and rushes out to get scratched by the brambles. They'd have been good and wet on Tuesday afternoon. Actually, there's no mention in the PM report of anyone's blood under Lorraine's fingernails.' Caroline was reluctant to dwell on her own objection to the theory she was propounding and rushed on before Mitchell could seize on it. 'The wet weather would have made it easy for her to leave the house. The back staircase goes right down to the basement and no one would have been interested in looking out at the garden. They'd probably shut the curtains.'

Mitchell nodded. 'You know, Antonia wouldn't have risked all that much by being at the reception. If someone saw her she could always say her meeting had been cancelled and she'd decided to come on to join them all again. She made it too complicated. She'd have done better to have been there openly. Then she could have criticized Diane's taste in interior decoration without putting herself in danger.'

'And let her father rattle on to his heart's content about her lunch appointment. Have we got enough?'

'We've got an unidentified print on the bedhead, remember.'

'And can we get her for Donna too?'

'If we can connect her with a grey Escort – or if Donna recovers enough to tell us.'

After a tap at the door, Cranton and Guest reappeared, fifteen minutes to the second after they had been allowed to leave. 'The nicotine didn't help much,' Guest remarked gloomily.

Caroline grinned. 'It doesn't matter. The case broke whilst you were out.'

Mitchell left his doubts unspoken, afraid to quench this encouraging ray of hope.

*   *   *

158

Shakila was not displeased, as they left the Grants' house, to learn that her sergeant had expected this Saturday to be her day off. She had therefore booked herself on a half-day course and was being allowed to attend it. Having waved Jennifer off to Sheffield, she set off to Mitchell's office to report on her morning's work and collect her instructions for the afternoon. When she found no one there, her hopes of continuing to direct her own activities rose. However, she dutifully returned to the station sergeant's desk to ask where Mitchell was.

Magic was, as usual, monosyllabic. 'Out.'

'What am I supposed to do?'

'Use your nous.'

Shakila nodded and wandered out to the car park, following a devious train of thought. She could hardly let it get to the super's ears that Mitchell had left her at a loose end. That would not be good for a CI's reputation. She had no idea where Caroline or Clement might be. She could hardly waste an afternoon that she was being paid for, could she? It was just about noon. If she got a move on, she might catch Victor Grant's unfortunate staff before they departed to enjoy what was left of the weekend.

She climbed into the car – her own this time, the same make and in similar condition to Nick Felling's – and set off for the palatial offices of Victor Grant. She'd find some office junior, someone in too lowly a position to have to worry about the reputation of the company, and see what she could get him or her to gossip about.

She ignored the main gate, parking in a side street round the corner from it. Climbing out, she showed great concern about a scratch on the shabby paintwork on the Renault's bonnet. She had to wait only a couple of minutes before a man in Victor Grant overalls approached a side gate. He glanced at his watch, put out his cigarette with work-hardened fingers and made to enter unobtrusively. This was her man and her brief with him was her own. Get him talking about anything. She licked her finger and gave the offending scratch a rub as he passed, shrugging at him with a murmur of 'Flaming kids!'

He grinned at her. 'They usually want something shinier than that to spoil. Seems to me you should mend that with a new one.'

Shakila bridled. 'I've had this since I passed my test years ago. I'm attached to it.' She changed her expression to hopeful. 'You wouldn't be Mr Greenslade, would you?'

The man wrinkled his nose. 'We 'aven't no Greenslade to my knowledge. What was it about?'

Shakila looked worried. 'Oh sugar, I knew I should have written it down. I'll be in dead lumber with my boss.'

It seemed the man could identify with this. 'And me with mine if I gossip with girls in worktime.'

'You work all of Saturday?'

He nodded glumly. 'When I'm hard up I do, or if there's a complicated job on.'

Shakila produced her warrant card which immediately reassured him.

'Well, can't argue with that, can he? We've not had a break-in, have we?' He seemed pleased at the prospect. As she shook her head, another cheering thought struck him. 'Hey, it's not about this funeral do, is it?'

She nodded and the man considered, trying to be helpful. Then he stuck out his hand. 'Ted Hallesby, one of VG's mechanics. I'm right about your heap of scrap. Don't throw good money after bad.' When this made Shakila no more cheerful, he went on. 'I look after the firm's fleet of cars and lorries. Leastways, my boss does.'

Shakila was inspired. 'Oh, thank goodness. My second job here was some questions about the firm's transport. Tell you the truth, I'd rather ask one of the honest to goodness fettlers about it. They're less interested in covering up for the firm, watching their own backs – and half of the bosses don't see what's under their noses anyway.'

'Is it about that damaged Escort?'

'There you are, see? You're on the ball straight away. I shan't need the boss. I've just to confirm the details. You know, registration, exactly what damage was done, time it

160

was first noticed. You can imagine the stuff I need. The folk with the desk jobs hadn't much clue.'

'Well, they wouldn't have.' Amiably, he took Shakila into a grimy, glass-walled cubicle just inside the gate, where he answered her list of questions, going into considerable detail about the innards of his ailing car. Shakila understood very little of it. She scribbled fast, hoping that what she wrote would mean something to Clement.

'Will it take much putting right?'

He shook his head. 'Shouldn't think so. What'll take my boss's time is finding out what happened and who did it. He's livid. All the cars were supposed to be in the garage on Thursday night and they all were when we locked up and went home. It was funny, really. I was busy making a list of all the key-holders, to check with them. We thought we'd be in big trouble about it but Mr Grant came down here himself, just asked us the once about whether we'd done everything as usual and said he'd look into it himself. He even said the garage looked nice and clean and the fleet in good nick.'

'Well, he's right. It does. You couldn't run through that list of key-holders for me, could you?'

Hallesby obliged, counting on grimy-nailed fingers. 'Mr Grant hisself, me and Mr Gage – my boss – then Mr Conroy and Antonia and Mr Bates.'

'Mr Bates?'

'He's the brother-in-law of that bird as was done in at the funeral.'

'Yes, I know. I thought he was a bank manager.'

'Might be. Mr Grant's pally with him, anyway. They've both got a Morgan as they won't trust a garage with. They fettle 'em theirselves and use our equipment and tools. We don't mind. They never make no mess and only come on Sundays.'

Shakila thanked the man and made a note to ask Clement what a Morgan looked like. 'So why is your boss going to have to waste his time on sorting out the bashed-in Escort?'

161

'Because what Mr Grant says he'll do and what he does aren't always the same thing,' Ted Hallesby said darkly.

'And you say this was Thursday night?'

Shakila's tone was sharper than she had intended, and suddenly the man became less friendly. 'I don't want trouble here from you lot because of what I've said. Ask the top brass if you want any more. In fact . . .'

Shakila understood. 'Hallesby? Don't know anyone of that name.' She grinned at him and they parted in friendly fashion.

Mitchell sent Clement with Caroline to bring in Antonia Grant for further questioning. They found that she too had taken refuge in her office at the factory, arriving there just a couple of minutes after Shakila had departed.

Antonia dismissed her personal assistant and offered them seats. Caroline took the armchair in front of the huge desk and Clement went to fetch an upright chair from over by the window. Glancing out, he froze.

A pale blue Escort had been driven into the car park and a man wearing overalls climbed out and locked the driver's door. Clement asked, 'Before we begin, Miss Grant, could you tell me who is the man just leaving the blue Escort outside?'

She came to look and shrugged. 'One of the mechanics. I don't know his name.'

'Is it his car?'

'No, it's one of the firm's cars. It had a slight bump recently. I expect he's been checking it over.'

'Who drives it? Who was driving it when this small accident occurred?'

Antonia shook her head. 'I've no idea. Why do you want to know?'

'Our curiosity is endless. It's a habit of ours to ask questions.'

'Then you'd better ask whatever it is you've come to ask. I've got a meeting in half an hour.'

Clement had to admit that Miss Grant met their suspicions with great dignity. He supposed she had reason to. Daddy would have dealt with any problems she had had as a child. Money would have dealt with them when she became an adult. Now she would be convinced that a well-paid lawyer would relieve her of this one.

Having politely allowed Clement to have his say, she merely remarked, 'It's an interesting theory, but since it's the wrong one I think you'll have a lot of trouble proving it.'

Nevertheless, she rang her father's mobile telephone number to summon his assistance. Grant justified her trust in him. He arrived in golfing attire only eight minutes after his daughter's call, helped her into her coat and calmly assured her that her lawyer would be at the station almost as soon as she was. He was urbane and polite to Caroline and Clement. 'I realize you have your job to do, Constable Clement, Constable Jackson. Since my daughter is not capable of the crime she is accused of –'

'Is being held on suspicion of.'

'However you like to express it. Since Antonia cannot have killed anyone, your evidence must all be circumstantial. I hope, when everything is cleared up, that your apology will be very humble.'

The two officers exchanged alarmed glances. Was the evidence very shaky? If the print on the bedhead let them down and nothing came of examining the car, they might be on rather unsafe ground. Caroline decided they had better get the car impounded right now.

'The light blue Escort parked outside, sir?'

'What about it?'

'We shall have to take it in and examine it. I hope that won't be too inconvenient.'

Grant smiled. 'Anything to assist. I think we can spare one.'

Clement blinked. 'How many blue Escorts have you got?'

'I think it's fourteen. I take it you won't be wanting them all.'

A wicked smile crept over both their faces as Clement

163

told him, 'I'm rather afraid that we will.' Now, even Victor Grant looked taken aback.

A few minutes later, the two officers were walking, one each side of Antonia, to the police car outside. Caroline leaned across to Clement to mutter, 'You'll be the one to tell forensic what you've taken on for them!'

Towards the end of the afternoon, Mitchell answered the telephone on his desk. Magic's voice announced, 'Anonymous call for you. Do you want it?'

Mitchell wanted anything that might throw further light on the case. 'Yes . . .'

Magic, having got his question answered, cut off Mitchell's intended and more gracious reply. After a series of clicks, Magic added, 'You're through,' and the mystery caller could be heard clearing his throat.

'I want to hear what you've got to tell me, name or no name,' Mitchell began, 'but you must realize that information you give won't be much use if it's anonymous.'

'It must be if you want to hear it.'

Accepting the logic of this, Mitchell waited. To his surprise, after a few seconds, the caller gave in. 'If anything I say helps you to pin anything on the dirty sod, it'd be worth anything he could do to me.'

Mitchell assumed a conversational tone. 'Which particular sod would that be?'

'It'd be Victor Grant. The bastard's been sniffing round my kid and she's only sixteen. Now I've got summat on him, though. Wednesday morning, I went to the Gleneagles Hotel, south side of Bradford. Been sent to deliver swatches to some biddy who was ordering new table linen for the upstairs restaurant. Saw VG there.'

'What time was this?'

'Nine thirtyish. He was getting into a car outside. I ducked out of his way, smartish.'

'Why?'

'I knew he'd be annoyed to be seen. He'd have been

164

with one of his lady friends and he wouldn't want to have to explain things to me.'

'Any particular lady friend?'

The man laughed. 'He isn't very particular! Did hear as he was having a bit of a fling with Antonia's future mother-in-law but it'd hardly have been her.'

'Did you know he was back from Germany?'

'No, I was surprised. He thought things would drag on. At least, that's what he said. I'm not saying different – except to you. I've a lot to lose if he thinks my gossip set his wife on to him again. Bet he wishes he hadn't come back early this time. They'll find out he missed that funeral on purpose now and that should give him some aggro from a few people. Now you know he was in England, he'll be hounded by you folk as well as the family.'

There was a pause as both men considered their position. It was broken by a further capitulation. 'OK, we'll play it your way. Name of Smith. No, I'm not beggaring about. It's Xavier Smith which sort of picks me out from all the others.'

Mitchell trod carefully. 'You were only doing your job when you saw your employer on Wednesday morning. You'd only be doing your duty in telling the truth when I call you in for questioning, wouldn't you? I need to check his alibi with you.'

'OK. What does he say?'

Mitchell laughed. 'You can't do it that way round. If I tell you what he's told us, you might confirm it, to keep your job.'

'Are you saying you suspect . . .' The man's tone revealed his delight.

'I'm saying nothing, except that we've got forty-odd stories to check up on, and the more you can tell us, the better it'll be for you if you ever come up against us yourself. Where are you?'

'I'm actually sitting on your car park wall, and it's bloody cold.'

'Come on in, then. I'll have the coffee on.'

*   *   *

165

Xavier Smith had only just departed when Shakila bounced, rather than walked into Mitchell's office. She refused to meet his eye as she enumerated her various reasons for taking herself off to Victor Grant's factory premises. 'I'd looked for you everywhere I could think of and . . .'

Mitchell bit his lip. He had been out on a limb himself too often as a DC to wish to reprove her. 'Just get on with what you've got to tell me.'

Hopefully, she raised her eyes and described her conversation with Victor Grant's assistant mechanic, omitting his name, as she had promised him. She was less than pleased to discover that her DCI knew already about the damaged car.

Mitchell was equally upset to find another suspect with a credible motive and a possible opportunity to kill Lorraine Conroy. He sent Shakila off to write her report. Then sensibly, deciding that cheerful company and calories would put him in the right frame of mind to grapple with this surfeit of suspects, he set off for the canteen. There he found Colin Warren sitting behind a pint mug of thick tea and a plate full of crumbs.

Armed with his own supply of comfort food and coffee, Mitchell joined his ex-colleague. 'Scrounging information – or just patronizing the best and cheapest restaurant in town?'

Warren considered. 'It probably is, and I've already put in enough hours on the beat to keep the privilege. I was going to pop up to your office before I left but I'd rather talk to you here than staring at your poor, over-pruned ivies.'

Mitchell hastily swallowed his mouthful of sausage sandwich. 'You've got something on the case? Or did you want to pick my brains about one of yours?'

'Just wanted to know how far on you were. I'll be glad to see you nail this villain. Lorraine was one of the people this miserable world needed to have around.'

'Unless you were part of her family. She created mayhem of various kinds for them.' Providence had been kind to him. Here was someone who both knew his victim and understood his problems. 'I don't feel I've got to grips with her as a person in the way I usually have with the victim at this stage of a case. I've listened to a lot of complaints about her and heard a lot of family members playing down her faults or exaggerating them according to how much she had inconvenienced them. You met her in a different context. How did you come to take her on? Did she answer an advertisement?'

Warren shook his head. 'She was a friend of a friend. Someone I did a job for was in that drama group she belonged to. A couple of times, for a joke, he told me, she'd come along to a rehearsal in disguise, just to see how long she could get away with it. The first time, it was almost an hour. The second, of course, they were prepared for. I was beginning to think of taking someone on and this all sounded very useful.

'When I mentioned it to my ex-client, he said Lorraine was looking for a job because she needed the money and that she would probably jump at the chance to do something so offbeat as working for me. She was and she did.'

'Did you like her?' Mitchell took another huge bite and sat back to listen.

'Yes and no. I didn't know about the drinking, as I've told you. That might explain her . . .' He frowned as he sought the right word. 'She wasn't unstable exactly, but she was unpredictable. She was reliable in the job because it excited her, but, as a friend, she might have got tired of you. She wasn't dependable, didn't keep her men long – by her own account.'

'That wasn't her fault in Mark Conroy's case. And then, according to our information, Philip's father ran out of her life and his responsibilities before the child was born. Maybe, by the time Nick Felling came along, she couldn't stand the tension of waiting till he let her down too.'

Colin Warren laughed. 'You seem to me to have got your head round her pretty well. I don't entirely agree with

167

your assessment though. She knew exactly what people were saying about her, seemed almost proud of it.'

'But it might have been a case of attacking herself before someone else did it. Still, maybe I'm over-simplifying things. You seem to have got on well with her.'

'Well, she certainly opened up to me.'

'Maybe she had you lined up as number four.'

Mitchell noted Warren's blush as he shook his head. 'I wasn't in the right league. She boasted how many people she had something going with.'

'Who?'

'Well, if she was to be believed, the little surgeon whose wife, however much he loved her, left him a bit, well, uncatered for. Then there was a sub-editor with the *Clarion* and Victor Grant – oh, and one of you lot!'

Mitchell turned back to his plate and was disappointed to find it empty. 'That'd be a complication I can do without. The girl, Donna, says that one of Lorraine's friends bought her Chanel No. 5. Any idea who that would be?'

'Well, they could all afford it – except the copper, of course.'

'Are you serious about that? Do you mean someone in this station?'

There was a pause before Warren answered. 'She didn't say.'

Chapter Eleven

Mitchell had jibbed at sending a third member of his available team on yet another trip to Manchester and was hoping to check the travel arrangements of Antonia Grant's Tuesday client by telephone. Clement, in despondent mood, had warned him that he would waste as much time pressing buttons and listening to canned music as it would take to drive along the M62 and back.

He had misjudged the airport authorities. The junior who took Mitchell's call sounded young but intelligent. She wondered aloud who would be the best person to approach. 'I can see on the computer that a Mr Shute was booked to fly to Perth from Manchester with a three-hour stop in Singapore. Whether he actually flew shouldn't be difficult to check. I could ring you back in half an hour if –'

Mitchell cut into her assurances with his thanks, hoping he didn't sound too impatient. 'The next request is a bit more complicated. Another journey to check, this time from Germany.' The girl assured him it would be no trouble. 'The passenger's name is Grant, Victor Albert Grant. We know already, in this case, that a passenger flew, under that name, from Germany last Wednesday morning.' He gave the girl details of the airport, time and airline used. He tapped his pencil on the desk as the girl read the details back to him from the notes she had made.

'So, what else do you need?'

'We need to be sure it really was Mr Grant. If I fax you a photograph . . .'

The youngster apparently felt this was outside her brief. 'I think you'd better speak to Mr Drinkelp.'

Mitchell felt the draught of his guardian angel's wing. 'That's an unusual name. Would it happen to be Roman Drinkelp from this side of the Pennines?'

'Well, he's definitely got a Yorkshire accent and his initial's R. His voice doesn't fit his name.'

So, the gods were on his side. 'I think he'll turn out to be an old schoolmate of mine.'

'I'll put you through, then, and I won't forget to get back to you about Mr Shute.'

The girl was happy again.

Although he had to endure three minutes or so of shapeless muzak before renewing his acquaintance with his former friend, by the time the call was finished Mitchell was happy too.

It was disappointing that the forensic evidence in the case was so inconclusive, in particular the fingerprints. Of the forty-four people present at the party on Tuesday night, no fewer than six had left prints on the bed and most of them had an innocent-seeming explanation.

Mitchell enlarged on the situation at the evening briefing. 'Obviously, the Bateses' prints are all over, including on the bed.'

'Well, they must have been in there after the cleaning woman had done her stuff then,' Jennifer cut in. 'The daily woman said she'd scoured that room especially, because, as she so tactfully reminded us, she thought it might be needed.'

'I suppose you use a spare room for storing things you only need occasionally, so they'd have been . . .'

Mitchell grinned. 'Thank you, Adrian. We can follow that deep thought to its conclusion, although I think the thoroughness of the cleaning might have been exaggerated if it was called into question. I can imagine Diane Bates being pretty unpleasant with people who don't come up to scratch for her. Nick Felling and Philip Conroy quite reasonably claim they touched the bedhead when they were getting Lorraine into bed and the cleaner, thorough or otherwise, left one of her own. There was a thumbprint of Antonia's that's a bit more compromising in view of the claims that she's made.'

Caroline raised a hand. 'I've been thinking about Toni Grant. She told me she was in Philip's flat to collect some shoes on Thursday afternoon. If Donna did ring there, hoping her brother would help her, Toni might have offered to lend some of her own things. Then she'd have had keys to open the firm's garage. The staff would have gone by five, or not long after.'

Mitchell considered. 'That would be cutting it a bit fine for the play in Manchester.'

Caroline nodded. 'I suppose so. Have we let her go?'

'We've let both Grants go but we're keeping obbo. So, what about Victor? He certainly flew back from Hanover on Tuesday, not Wednesday. He admits it now that we've got double evidence.'

'Someone else besides the VG rep?'

Mitchell grinned at Clement's show of familiarity with the file. 'Unfortunately for friend Victor, the colleague he swapped tickets with made a thorough nuisance of himself on the trip back on Wednesday, so everyone remembers his complaints. I sent them a photograph. Apparently the cabin staff thought the man in our picture looked the kind of passenger they liked looking after. The one they got certainly wasn't Victor. But, if he's our man, what would his motive be?'

'Lorraine was maybe threatening to reveal everything if he didn't give her a well-paid job in his firm.'

Mitchell raised an eyebrow at Shakila. 'How have you managed to keep quiet for so long? It's certainly all he'd deserve. He's made an ungentlemanly offer of all the details concerning his amour of Tuesday night. Says he'll have no trouble getting her to admit everything.'

'But, for Donna? What's he got against her?'

Mitchell shook his head and conceded that he had no

171

suggestions, though he had a final piece of news. 'Donna, by the way, is now conscious, on and off.'

'That's good news.' They had all perked up and the comment came as a chorus.

'For the family, it certainly is, but it's not much use for us. She has no recollection of making a phone call and no memory of her accident at all.'

The thumbprint on Diane's guest room bedhead was brought to the attention of Antonia Grant's lawyer. He claimed that, whether or not that particular print was his client's, she could not possibly remember each trivial family visit over a period of months. Since Mrs Bates and Miss Grant got on so well it would be very odd if at some time they had not gone together round the Bateses' beautiful house. Antonia thought that she did remember now that, soon after she and Philip first became friendly, she had been shown some of Diane's treasures. The lawyer almost persuaded Diane that she had given Antonia a lecture on the works of Fabergé. 'That was when the thumb mark must have been left.'

Mitchell produced an irate Mrs Andrews who declared yet again that she polished 'every skerrick of wood in Mrs B's house every single week!' And she had definitely given the place an extra special 'do' on Monday, as she'd made perfectly clear last time she was asked, the day before the funeral. She had taken great care in the guest room because, as she once more explained, 'I thought Mrs Felling might be in need of a bit of a lie down.' It took Caroline some time to assure her that no one thought she had skimped on her work and to calm her sufficiently to sign her second statement.

The airline official's confirmation that Mr Shute had made a late-afternoon booking and that he had travelled to Australia from Manchester as scheduled was reproduced. Mitchell now had Mr Shute's personal confirmation that he had left Miss Grant at three minutes to two. This proved, said the assiduous lawyer, that his client had indeed perverted the truth but only to get out of a trying family occasion without hurting any feelings.

'How thoughtful,' Mitchell had commented.

'Also,' the lawyer had explained ingratiatingly, 'Miss Grant is having second thoughts about marrying Mr Conroy and she's trying to ease out gently, by not being at his side in every crisis.'

A flake of paint found on Donna's borrowed anorak matched exactly the paintwork on the damaged car from the fleet of fourteen that had come from Victor Grant Ltd. Why, demanded the indefatigable lawyer, should the chairman's daughter not have driven any of the cars belonging to her father's business? This time no one could be persuaded to come forward and testify to having done – or not done – a thorough cleaning job just before the weekend. The car maintenance team valued their jobs.

However, no prints on that vehicle could be traced back to Antonia Grant. When her lawyer left, Mitchell was clearing away the papers to which they had both referred when another idea occurred to him. Antonia Grant had admitted to her lawyer that her engagement to Philip Conroy was not, as far as she was concerned, a determination to marry him. Suppose Philip already knew that she was cooling off?

He smiled to himself as the phrase came into his mind. It seemed unlikely that this cold couple could lose any more heat without freezing. Still, Philip might think that his present position in Grant's business and his future promotion prospects depended on the wedding taking place. Had he considered his mother an obstacle to this?

There was a tap on the door, followed by Shakila's head appearing round it. He invited the rest of her in. 'How did you know I needed someone to bounce an idea around with?'

Shakila calmly seated herself without stating the purpose of her visit. The opportunity he was offering her was more important. 'What idea's that?' When Mitchell explained, she blinked. 'That's what I've been wondering. Philip Conroy seems to have been let off the hook. He

173

accepted the news of his mother's death, even her murder, so calmly.'

'Does that make him guilty?'

'I suppose not. Murder doesn't leave you calm.'

'That's personal experience, I presume.'

She ignored this. 'Nicholas Felling told Clement that Philip had given up trusting life to give him a fair deal.'

'But that's only an opinion. In any case, it's a good job that everyone in that frame of mind doesn't become murderous. And what about Donna? He seems genuinely to be on very good terms with his sister. Clement thinks it doesn't seem put on. He said it's evident in their casual exchanges.'

'So, he did one and not the other?'

'Certainly, he could have done. Philip and Victor Grant alibi each other for Thursday afternoon. Even if they're both being honest, it's not very firm. They wouldn't have spent every minute in the same office, in sight of one another.'

Shakila preferred an intrigue. 'What if they're in league?'

Mitchell shook his head impatiently. 'Why should they be?'

'So that Philip could be next in line for Edgar's money after Lorraine. Then he could invest some of it in the firm, or if not, he'd be able to keep Toni in the manner to which she's accustomed. He'd have had a good case against Nicholas Felling, even if it had struck him that Felling might inherit.'

'And that wasn't what he expected.'

They sat in silence for some seconds, then Mitchell grinned. 'Shakila, how many cells are there downstairs?'

She stared at him. 'Eight, aren't there? Why?'

'Just go down and see if there's one we've left empty. If you can find one, I might let you bring Conroy in. Otherwise, it'll have to be your house!'

Mitchell had reached the point where he could tolerate no more of either his office or his colleagues. Certainly, he did

174

not dislike either but he suspected he would get no further with his thinking about the case until he had had a change of company and surroundings. In any case, it was time his children were reminded that they had a father.

He was not expected and the delight of the four youngsters as they ran out to meet him was almost sufficient therapy in itself. For a few minutes, he gave them his full attention. They escorted him into the hall, then gathered round as he sat on the stairs to remove his outdoor shoes. Virginia came into the hall, grinned at him over the heads of their offspring and asked if he had eaten. When he shook his head she disappeared into the kitchen.

The twins were halfway through their preparations for bed and Michael, standing on the end of his pyjama trouser leg, was red-faced with frustration because they refused to pull up to his waist. Before Mitchell could intervene, Caitlin had dealt with her brother without interrupting their conversation, which seemed, to his amusement, to be about how to choose a future spouse. Caitlin, with her usual common sense, was apparently already looking out for a hard-working fellow who never got drunk and who would help her with the children. Mitchell hoped she would be of the same mind when the question became more relevant. Having had his pyjamas sorted out for him, Michael prepared to make a contribution. He chattered less than his siblings so that when he spoke they usually heard him out. He was their only fair-haired child with the same blue eyes as his twin, but he was solidly built and placid. He watched life rather than participating in it, but the watching was done with keen interest.

'I'm going to marry Zoe,' he announced, 'because she's the best girl to play with. When I grow up, I'm going to be a knight. I'll have a big shield to defend us against the terrorists. Knights have to wear armour to fight. I'll take it off when I've won, so that we can play and eat our dinner.' A thought occurred that amused him. 'If I kept it on, Zoe could put my food through the vizor like posting a letter.'

Mitchell, with solemn interest, asked, 'So, you've definitely settled on Zoe?'

Michael nodded. 'Yes, because she gave me a robot birthday card, but . . .' His brow wrinkled. 'Zoe wants to marry Patrick. She's silly, because he keeps getting into trouble with Mrs Dennison.' Caitlin, self-appointed protector of Michael, glared round as the others began to giggle.

Declan spoke up with the responsible air of the eldest. 'You shouldn't choose a wife just for good looks, should you? Even good-looking girls can be cruel to animals and nasty. A few days after you've watched her to see if she's good-looking, you should wait another few days to see if she's kind and loving. Actually, I think ten's a bit early for a girlfriend, but I think you should start looking in secondary school.'

Mitchell kept a straight face with difficulty. 'Well, it's a good idea to begin considering early, I suppose. You're married for a long time.'

Declan looked pleased with this support from his father. 'I agree. I don't think you should get divorced once you're married, but getting separated is all right because it helps to sort things out. If one of the persons gets bored, that's a tricky question.' He considered in silence for a few seconds and Mitchell was surprised to see that the others waited for his pronouncement. 'If they split up, the one with the children should be given a child-minder.'

Mitchell could contain himself no longer and guffawed. 'Was that your mother's suggestion?'

Declan, looking offended, paused again, then decided, 'No. She doesn't seem to mind looking after us.'

Mitchell turned to his other twin who had been uncharacteristically silent. 'Are you going to get married, Sinead?'

She gave him a look of withering scorn. 'I don't know, do I? I'm only five. It's ladies who get married. I'm not going to be a lady. They have to do the ironing when boys and girls go to the park.'

Mitchell allowed himself the luxury of putting the twins

to bed before reporting to the kitchen for his meal. Michael, as usual, had to be half-carried upstairs. He would have been mortified to be given an earlier bedtime than his twin, but by the time she showed any sign of wilting, Michael was always practically comatose.

Sinead was now elaborating on the unfairness of having to go upstairs when the others were going to talk to Daddy over supper. 'No, they aren't,' he told her. 'I'm going to talk to Mummy about my work, Kat's going to water the garden for me and Declan's going to do his homework.'

Michael roused himself to mutter, 'I'm a good waterer.'

'You're a very splendid morning waterer, but now you're both going to bed. Not another word.' He gave them the look with which he could silence even Shakila, then returned to the kitchen with less trepidation than had been usual.

Ginny was not a good cook, but she had recently undertaken a course at the local college in an attempt to improve matters. Mitchell suspected that the comments of their forthright children, when they became aware that their own meals compared unfavourably with those of other families, had had some part in this decision. He had had the sense not to say so. Today, Mitchell decided, Ginny's casserole was interesting. It fell short of being delicious but was certainly palatable. She was not yet sufficiently confident in this field to demand praise and they both ate without comment on the food.

'What,' he demanded, 'have you been doing to the kids?'

'Doing to them?'

'They've all decided to leave home and get married. They've been working out what sort of people would be suitable candidates.'

Virginia's face cleared. 'Oh, that's because Alex rang to tell us he and Charlotte have got engaged. Choosing their own partners makes a nice change. What I've had all afternoon is arguments about bridesmaids' dresses from the girls – not that they've been invited to wear them yet

177

– and declarations from our eldest that he won't be a page boy even if we double his pocket money.'

Mitchell grinned. 'Well, thank the Lord for that.'

Virginia demanded to be entertained by his progress with the case. 'I've done my homework, read all the papers. Your victim's a lush who collapsed at a funeral wake. She's had three relationships that have left her with a grown-up son and a young daughter. She's put to bed while the rest continue with their fun until someone sneaks up and suffocates her. Who did it?'

'She wasn't a lush, though she did have a drink problem. You seem as genned-up as we are, so you can give me just as neat a summary of all your suspects.'

This kind of conversation was, Mitchell knew, one of her compensations for the long hours of acting as a single parent. It was also often the source of a fresh approach or a new thought that was useful to the team. He waited with some interest for her suggestions.

'Donna. She's adolescent, embarrassed, probably squeamish. How would you like to clean up the unspeakable messes made by an incapable drunk?'

'You put the child first? Most of the team are up in arms because we're considering her at all.'

'She's not a child. And she's got most to gain.'

'Edgar Smith's money, you mean?'

'No. I mean she gets her life back.'

'That's what Nick Felling wanted for her – rescue from that awful life. He wanted custody for her protection and the pleasure of her company.'

Virginia tried again. 'What about Lorraine's sister?'

'According to what various people have told us, Diane Bates has always been jealous of Lorraine who was the father's favourite – popular and entertaining in spite of all her shortcomings. Diane seems reserved and snobbish and generally disliked. She's furious that Lorraine was left most of their father's money.'

'I don't blame her. I've not much time for a law that discriminates against sensible, hard-working people and lets irresponsible good-timers collect. Was there much for the grown-up son?'

'Something but not a lot.'

Virginia spooned the last of the casserole on to Mitchell's plate and he produced well-simulated gratitude. 'He's attached to the Grant girl, according to the *Clarion*. They won't be able to have a slap-up wedding for a while now. It might make Victor Grant's sales go down if . . .' She stopped speaking as Mitchell shook his head.

'I'm sure she didn't fancy Lorraine Conroy as a mother-in-law, but I get the impression that romance is dying on its feet anyhow. He seems a cold fish – very calm and matter-of-fact about his mother and hardly the dashing young lover either.'

Virginia considered what she had been told as she removed the casserole dish and replaced it with an apple pie. Mitchell insisted on making the custard and Virginia agreed immediately. 'I'll let you. If even two grains stick together you call it a lump. I shouldn't be bothering with this college course. It never claimed to make me capable of pleasing a perfectionist.'

He put a finger over her lips. 'I want to make custard, like I make coffee, because a man should have one or two things he can do better than his wife.'

'You could be an expert washer up.'

'Why should I? We've got four children.'

Virginia returned to the more interesting topic. 'What have you got against the poor surgeon? He only tried to help you.'

'Quite a lot.' He elaborated on Scott's experiments and, as he had expected, she demanded details of Mrs Scott's illness which he could not provide.

She promised to do that piece of homework for him. 'Do you seriously suspect him? You know he's been exploiting the youngsters, of course – but of killing Lorraine? Unless – you don't think Donna was one of his volunteers?'

'Bloody hell! We never thought of that one. It could even be interfering with her recovery from her injuries. I'll get someone on to it pronto.'

179

'Jen told me you're chasing Victor Grant. You'll be everyone's butt if he turns out to be shiny clean, the pure philanthropist the *Clarion* keeps telling us he is.'

There was a pause as Mitchell carefully measured custard powder and poured boiling water. Eventually, he said, 'We both know better than that.'

'He's a ladies' man, isn't he?'

'Why do you ask?'

'I'm not asking, I'm telling. He's got a lot to tempt them with – some types, anyway.'

'He's a nancy!'

'You mean he's ageing in the way lucky men do and you won't – hair silver but still thick, skin lined but tans easily, still well muscled and lean.'

He grinned 'You sound smitten yourself.'

Virginia wrinkled her nose. 'He's not a gentleman.'

'And I am?'

'I'm not committing myself. You wouldn't tell all to save your own skin though.'

He stopped joking and stared at her. 'Did Jen tell you that?'

'No. I deduced it from all the smirking pictures he gets the *Clarion* to publish. I didn't know he had but I could have told you he would.'

'So, what else does your women's intuition tell you?'

'Well, it's not intuition exactly, but I read something that I think is true.'

Mitchell groaned. 'I'm sure you're going to read it to me.'

'Just stir the custard and listen. It was in some novel, I think, not a textbook. One of the characters said that to commit murder you had to be one-idea'd. As long as you have a variety of interests you can't care about any one of them to the point of murder. It's when you have all your eggs in one basket that you lose your sense of proportion.'

'So, who does that make your man?'

Mitchell helped himself to more than his share of pie as his wife chased her fancy notions. Well dowsed with his own custard, it should be edible. He blinked. 'This could have been made by my mother – hey! It wasn't, was it?'

She shook her head. 'My own mother taught me to make good pastry. It was what I used to put into it that you didn't like. And, to answer your question, I suppose Neville Scott seems to be a man with one idea – to save his wife.'

'You were calling him our "poor surgeon" a minute ago. Anyway, he's dedicated his career to saving life. Would he sacrifice one to save another? . . . I suppose he might for his own wife. Swearing the hippocratic oath, if they still do that, doesn't guarantee your morals. He's risked the lives of we don't know how many young kids.'

'What charge will he have to face for that?' Without waiting for an answer, Virginia went on, 'He did try to check up on them and take care of them.'

'He'd have to, to save his own reputation.'

'He'd already lost that. If one of those boys had become seriously ill, even with a complaint totally unconnected with the drugs, he'd sue Scott and the whole world would know. They'd soon give up regular small payments in exchange for a huge court settlement.'

'Unless he chose them all as carefully as young Craig Potter. He's begging us not to take proceedings.'

'OK. Deadlock with Scott. Besides, what could he possibly have to gain from attacking Donna?'

Mitchell shook his head. 'We've done that one. Now we're going round in circles.'

Virginia licked the last of Mitchell's custard from her spoon, then asked, 'Either of your young lovers?'

'We've had Toni in but we had to let her go. Her prints on the bed were only one set of several and we'd nothing much else on her. We've nothing at all on Philip. Victor Grant's been in for questioning too. I've sent a PC to see if his lady friend confirms all he's told us about Tuesday afternoon and evening.'

Virginia began to clear the table. 'All right, you've had all my ephemeral ideas. What material evidence are you following up?'

Mitchell counted the matters currently being dealt with on stubby fingers. 'I've got some uniforms tracking down how many people have a key to Victor Grant's factory garage. There is an official list but it seems that all manner of folk have had themselves one cut. It's got to be someone who had access to one of the firm's cars. We started at the top but no one's saying anything. The staff aren't going to risk their jobs. I'm going to have to dream up the right questions to ask Diane Bates. She reported a few items missing which her husband didn't.'

'Maybe Donna's guess was right and they were sold to pay for the funeral bash.'

'Bother you, woman! That's another job you've found for me. Anyway, I should be having this discussion with the super, not you.'

Virginia tossed her head. 'Rubbish! If you'd shared all your mad ideas with your various supers over the years, you'd have been sacked long ago. If I didn't screen what you say to them, we'd be on the streets.'

Mitchell glanced at his watch. 'We will be anyway if I don't get back. You know about as much as I do now. Throw me a new idea as a reward.'

'All right. Out of all the people you've met in connection with Lorraine Conroy, pick the most ordinary and respectable and prove it's him or her. Now I'm going to chase Declan and Kat to bed so buzz off.'

The telephone rang. Virginia picked up the receiver, listened, then handed it to Mitchell.

'Sir, it's Smithson. Victor Grant's given me the slip. I'm terribly sorry. He was –'

'Leave it, Smithson. I'm sure it wasn't your fault. Let's just find him.' He leapt into his car and roared off.

Caroline had spent her afternoon wondering how to break the news to Cavill that she would not be available to play the piano at his oldies' concert that evening. She had been astonished but relieved to receive the message that Magic Powers handed to her. Things were more or less under control and she was free to enjoy the rest of what should have been a day off.

She had spent the late afternoon attending to some much-neglected domestic tasks before reporting early to the huge church. It had become the home of various of Cloughton's amateur groups for both rehearsals and performances, which helped with its upkeep. If Cavill had his way, it would help with the organ fund. She found her husband haranguing a scared-looking cub reporter from the *Clarion*, as the orchestra members prepared their instruments and began to take their places.

'There's a whole different ethos here. How dare you make patronizing remarks about these players? They have a passion for their music which is what really matters. If there's no passion, there's no music and they have plenty of both. Just look at their faces. I'd rather conduct them than an over-coached, technically almost-perfect posh school orchestra, whose hearts aren't in their playing but whose reputation is invested in soulless scraping and blowing.'

Caroline spared a moment to sympathize with the young man and to wonder how these opinions of Cavill's would appear in print. With the press suitably subdued, Cavill turned to his players and Caroline hurriedly took her place at the piano.

The programme was neither highbrow nor ambitious. Some of the orchestra members played 'by ear', by which they meant that they could vamp along with a tune if they knew it. For concerts, as for their last rehearsal the previous night, discreetly placed friends of Cavill bolstered each section. The orchestra's reaction was not grateful. 'They don't do things like we do.' Caroline grinned to herself. You could say that again.

Having defended his players so stoutly, Cavill's remarks to them were not all kind, but his tone was mild and his smile broad. Her hands playing automatically, Caroline looked around her, missing Edgar Smith's white thatch that had used to interrupt the back row of shiny domes. She was well entertained.

Under cover of an arrangement of nursery rhyme tunes came a growl from the double bass player. 'My grandson plays this at the music centre and he's only seven!'

A cellist stopped playing to turn and smile sweetly at him. 'We've had this argument before, Ernie. We aren't too proud to perform good tunes just because they're simple, are we?' The string section concentrated once more on its duties. Their bows swept around the notes, disturbing the dust, and heavily veined hands, their fingers trembling against the frets, created an unintentional vibrato.

Most of the string players were ladies whose batwing upper arms sagged unbeautifully. Caroline made a mental note to suggest to Cavill that a rule of long sleeves should be added to the present free and easy uniform of anything black or white.The bows continued sawing on the strings, moving only an inch or two either way and producing strangled yelps. Cavill thanked providence when Gertrude McKintosh dropped her bow. Seeing her glare in his direction, he realized that he should have thanked Tom Wibsey, sitting behind her, who had disabled her for the two bars of demi-semi-quavers she could never manage. The two fudged bars he could have borne, but Gertrude, having taken extra time to fit in the recalcitrant notes, then played the rest of the piece approximately two bars later than the rest of the orchestra. This friend of his, who played in the Hallé Orchestra, mimed an apology to the old lady, Cavill wondered whether the incident was serendipity or whether Tom had planned this ruse for the performance.

Under cover of the smattering of clapping, as the piece finished, the first violin creaked to her feet, leaning forward to address Cavill. 'May I make a suggestion?' Without waiting for permission, she continued. 'If we get an encore for this next piece, could we play with plucked strings?'

His players had no patience with the notion that a last rehearsal was definitive. If helpful ideas occurred to them in the middle of an actual performance, then that was when they had to be suggested. Cavill was happy to agree with this one. There would be a better chance of the audience recognizing the tune, even though, by then, most of the instruments would need retuning.

The piece finished. To his relief, no one thought the volume of applause justified a repeat. There were smiles all round, some smug and satisfied, some sheepish.

For 'Hymn of Joy', a travesty of the last movement of Beethoven's Choral symphony, played in Cloughton, at least, at a funereal adagio, the whole orchestra was required. As they prepared themselves, Caroline sat, mesmerized by the reflection of the old church's once-magnificent, now peeling roof reflected in the bell of the euphonium resting on old Walter Denby's frail shoulder.

At the end of this item, Cavill allowed his drummer an improvisation on the timpani – chiefly, Caroline suspected, because he had no way of stopping her. This time it failed to happen and he saw that she had dropped one of her sticks. They waited as she grovelled on the floor for it. Cavill glanced at his violinist friend but Tom sat too far from the percussionist to be responsible this time. Annie was actually a good drummer. She didn't so much play the timps as dance with them. Her antics were not self-advertisement. There were no glances around to see who was watching. She was totally and absorbedly taken up into the rhythm.

As she waited, Caroline wondered what Cavill's proficient and obliging friends were making of the proceedings and what the busily scribbling young journalist was writing about them. Her stick retrieved, the anorexic percussionist gave an approving pat to her pot-bellied instrument and went into a frenzied roll, her moment of glory. Caroline was sure that the climax to her performance would one day be the rattle of her skeleton as her disconnected bones fell on each other to the floor.

With Beethoven successfully rendered, the players turned to their arrangement of Beatles songs. 'Which time round?' whispered the borrowed viola player to Caroline as they launched into 'When I'm sixty-four'.

She giggled. 'I keep imagining a huge fairy-tale creature stuck in an orchestra pit, roaring because the oldies are poking him with their instruments. I didn't know you could make a sound like that with a flute.' She stopped laughing and bit her lip in compunction as Cavill frowned her into silence. Not all these old people were deaf.

Cavill was annoyed with his wife. It was bad enough having to deal with jumped-up, uninformed reporters without Caroline joining the detractors of these vulnerable old folk. He continued to glare at her until he saw that she was sufficiently ashamed of herself. Satisfied, he encouraged his members into their next piece, hoping that they would remember his gentle haranguing at the last rehearsal and do themselves a little more justice. 'No note ends precisely,' he had told them. 'Each instrument leaves off when it decides to. Has playing in unison gone out of fashion? You seem to think a rest is when those who are watching me stop half a beat late and the rest stop on the next note, just as the first lot start playing again. It gives a curious but, I suppose, interesting impression – but not quite as effective as the silence the composer intended. And, Vic, you're coming through too strongly. The trumpet isn't supposed to dominate the section. Can you tone it down a bit?'

He often reprimanded his experts to soften the more necessary criticisms of his regular players. He wondered, though, if that particular remark had been wise and hoped the orchestra's generous sponsor had not been too put out.

His heart sank as the repeat he had reluctantly sanctioned was struck up a third time by the brass. Half the other players joined them. The rest sat looking bewildered before striking up again one by one. Cavill had a mental picture of the audience behind him wiping its eyes – except those who'd used their handkerchiefs to stuff their mouths. Oh, well, it was all entertainment. He felt no indignation. The audience's mirth was spontaneous, not spiteful. Their applause would be warm and not mocking. The bulk of them were relatives of his players who had made time to come and encourage them.

Some had come as a tribute to the former glory of certain

instrumentalists who had been more than competent in the past and given genuine artistic pleasure. He hoped and believed that these players had lost some discrimination, along with a certain amount of hearing and even more manual dexterity. God grant that they didn't appreciate their deterioration and, when they played, heard the standard they remembered themselves achieving.

They were all startled as the obtrusive buzz of Caroline's mobile phone cut through the music. She slipped into the section of the old building that had been its Lady chapel before accepting her call. She heard Mitchell's voice. 'Sorry about this, but we need you back. Victor Grant seems to have given Smithson the slip. His wife can't help. He wouldn't say where he was going. They seem to have had strong words. He could be in bed with another lady, but, equally, he could be on a plane to somewhere where it's safer for him and the ladies are just as lovely. How nearly is your concert over?'

Caroline grinned to herself and tried to sound indignant. 'It's only halfway through!'

'I'm really sorry, Caroline, but we need all hands to track him –'

Now she laughed aloud. 'No. You only need mine. He's here at St Barnabas', blowing his brains out in the middle of Cavill's old folks' trumpet section. We'll keep him busy for you till Smithson turns up to reclaim him.'

Again, Cavill was annoyed, but this time not with Caroline. He knew he needed her as their pianist even more than he needed Victor Grant as their sponsor. He also understood that, during a murder enquiry, Caroline was never off duty. He watched her as she listened and her lips moved in reply. Then she put up a thumb to him to signal that she was not being called away. She reseated herself at the piano and the concert programme creaked along to its inevitable end.

Chapter Twelve

Having cleared his desk and attended to the heap of messages waiting for him after his stolen couple of hours at home, Mitchell allowed himself, for a minute or two, to play with Virginia's suggestion. He began a list of the people connected with the murder who were unlikely perpetrators, respectable or not.

Ought he to have sought out Philip Conroy's biological father? Who would be able to supply even his name now that Lorraine Conroy and Edgar Smith were dead? Had he paid enough attention to old Walter Denby? The old man's affection for all the members of Lorraine's family seemed quite genuine. What sort of people were generally considered to be above reproach? Not teachers, or even church ministers. The tabloids these days were full of their misdemeanours – and sometimes their grievous sins. Bank managers, perhaps?

Mitchell sat very still for a moment, studying his mental picture of the Bateses. Clement, when he first met them, had found it hard to believe that Diane was only thirty-seven. Barry might be older, of course. According to various statements in the file, he had been Diane's immediate superior when they became engaged. They seemed like a middle-aged couple. You could imagine that their children had grown up and left home. He pictured Barry Bates in his old-fashioned suits with their unflattering double-breasted jackets, his hair thinning and his chin that seemed in the process of being reabsorbed into his face. The face was unlined, though. He couldn't be more than fifty.

As usual, Ginny had fed him a useful idea. He began a

feverish hunt through the papers in the file, scattering them over his desk. He ignored the knock on his door.

After a second knock, his visitor came in without an invitation. 'I had hoped for a progress report, Benny. Still, if Mahomet won't come to the mountain . . .'

'Be quiet a minute!' Mitchell's distracted hand waved his superintendent to a chair. Carroll exchanged a glance with Jennifer, who had come in behind him. Both of them realized that Mitchell's discourtesy was unintentional, that he was not even aware of it. They sat for a few moments, watching him.

When his telephone rang, Mitchell had to remove a mountain of paper under which it was buried before he could pick up. 'Is it important, Magic?'

It seemed that it was. 'Mr Moxon? You're not the Smith family's solicitor. Ah, Nicholas Felling's . . . That's very interesting.'

There was a long pause, during which Carroll and Jennifer waited impatiently, able to make nothing of the high-pitched twittering emitted by Mitchell's receiver.

'Yes, I know that's the Bateses' bank. What's the short-fall? . . . Could you repeat that?' Mitchell grabbed a sheet of paper and stuck out a hand. 'Pen!'

It was supplied but Mitchell could see that this summary treatment of his superior officer was beginning to rankle with him. He sought a more respectful tone. 'Please don't break my train of thought, sir.' It was enough. The superintendent subsided, mollified.

Mitchell listened, scribbled, then thanked his caller. 'Don't contact the bank again until we've sent someone to see you.' This had apparently not been sufficiently grace-ful. 'Of course you have to. We won't keep you waiting. We'll get someone round as soon as possible.' He pushed his file aside, rested his chin in his hands and considered all the possible implications of the news he had just received. He became excited and beamed at Carroll who was getting to his feet.

The superintendent met the smile and punished Mitchell for his lack of respect. 'Barry Bates has been helping himself to Edgar Smith's money, expecting to be able to juggle the accounts he manages and make things right when it was eventually split between Lorraine Conroy and his wife.' It was not even a question.

Mitchell was resentful but resigned. He grinned ruefully at Jennifer. 'Oh well, I suppose, if the beggar wasn't reasonably quick on the uptake, he wouldn't be our super.'

He turned to Carroll. 'Mr Moxon wasn't so rash as to make an accusation at this stage . . .'

'But the money in Edgar Smith's account, having passed in and out of Lorraine Conroy's possession, doesn't amount to what Felling's lawyer has been led to expect.'

'It's not the amount Mr Smith mentioned in his will, by some considerable difference.'

The superintendent had reached the door. 'Send someone to bring Bates in. I'll ring the bank as soon as it opens again to warn them that someone's coming to ask questions, with my written authority to see the relevant accounts. You make Moxon bring his facts and figures to you.'

He left them and Jennifer too rose to go. 'Which of those orders is for me?'

Mitchell shook his head. 'Uniforms can do most of that – and we can't do any of it tonight, except get Bates down here. Give me a minute.' Three telephone calls put Carroll's orders into action and he turned back to his sergeant. 'It's childish, but I wish Moxon's could have waited to make their call till their own office opens again. Ginny gave me an idea and, believe it or not, I was just sorting through all this guff for some evidence in support of Bates being our villain. It would have been good to present the idea to the super before there was outside evidence.'

Jennifer was unsympathetic. 'You're right. It is childish. Why did they ring on a Saturday night anyway? They should be enjoying their weekend.'

'Apparently, Moxon's a personal friend of Felling's. He's trying to hurry things through so that father and daughter can set up home as quickly as possible. He discovered the discrepancies this morning when the bank and his own business were still in session but he only tracked Felling down an hour or so ago.'

Jennifer seemed worried. 'Anyhow, the fact that Barry Bates seems to have played fast and loose with someone else's money – and we haven't proved that yet – doesn't mean he killed our victim. Let's stop guessing and see what we've got.'

Mitchell accepted the reproof with a grin. 'Let's start with what we got from the Smiths' solicitor when we first looked into Edgar's will.' He pulled it out triumphantly from the chaos in front of him. 'Mr Robarts drew it up twenty years ago and there have been two adjustments since. The more recent one was about two years ago. All three versions gave Lorraine the largest share and, in the third, she basically inherits the lot. There are legacies of varying sizes but definitely minor sums to Diane, Nick, domestic and company staff and one or two charities.'

'Didn't someone say he left Felling the market value of what used to be his house?'

'Well, the value two years ago at this latest adjustment. According to Mr Robarts, Edgar had been nagging Lorraine to make a will for years. She just laughed and said she didn't care who inherited her debts.'

'Was she in debt?'

'On and off, Mr Robarts thinks – nothing serious. In the end, Edgar decided to tell Lorraine how he'd left things. Then she went with him quite willingly and made every-thing over to Nick, part for him outright and part in trust for Donna. You should know all this. It's in the file.'

She scowled at him. 'Pots and kettles! How much is missing?'

'In the region of a hundred and fifty grand. I wonder if there's any question of old Edgar being inaccurate in his assessments.'

Jennifer shook her head. 'Possible, I suppose, but he wasn't all that old, only in his sixties and an astute busi-nessman. His death was sudden too, not a gradual failing. We'd better check that he hadn't been speculating unwisely but he doesn't sound that sort from what all his family and friends have said. That might be Bates's story, though.' Another thought struck her. 'If Donna dies –'

'It looks from the latest report as though she won't, thank goodness.'

'I'm very pleased. But, if Donna had died, what would have happened to the money that her mother left in trust for her? Would that revert to Diane Bates?'

'You're a genius, Jen. You've just provided the first believable motive for an attack on Donna – though I'm not sure that is where the money would go. My jaundiced opinion is that the bloody government would find some pretext for claiming it.'

'Wouldn't Barry Bates be genned up on where money goes in what circumstances? He'd check up, surely, before risking something so potentially dangerous for himself.'

'It'd be more dangerous for him if people knew he'd been asking questions like that. Anyway, I think the attack on Donna was a last-minute panic measure. Whoever fielded her telephone call wouldn't have been expecting it. Barry Bates was in a panic. He and Diane had been hoping to have charge of Donna, in particular of Donna's money. Then she takes off, determined, presumably, to show her father how violently she is opposed to the Bateses' plans for her.'

'But she'd know that Felling wouldn't want her living apart from him. I know the Bateses lied to her, but surely she'd believe her father rather than them.'

'She was pretty traumatized before her uncle and aunt tried their takeover bid. She'd lived with a drunken mother, lost a well-loved grandfather, then her mother's killed before the funeral is properly over and she knows that someone actually meant to do it. I'm surprised on two counts – first that the girl hasn't turned into a raving lunatic and second that, as far as I know, the social services didn't come snooping round ages ago.'

'It's a very close family group in spite of its fractured structure. And the social services don't usually snoop. We've been glad of them before now.'

Mitchell held his hand out to have it slapped. When she ignored it, he returned to their potential villain. 'Barry Bates is the last person Donna would apply to. He was trying to separate her from her father.'

'But, until this financial crisis blew up, he hadn't wanted to take her in. She might well have thought of him as her ally against her aunt. Or, what if she rang her brother?'

Mitchell was puzzled. 'Go on.'

'Expecting him to be in his flat, which he wasn't. But running to Philip would be what Barry was expecting. Maybe he went there to find her.'

'How would he get in?'

'Philip's his nephew. He might possibly have a key – or Bates could have arrived while Toni Grant was there collecting her shoes . . .'

'And answered the phone, promising to meet Donna while Toni, because she'd been so well brought up, went into another room so as not to eavesdrop? Try again, Jen.'

'All right. Let's stop inventing and go back to what we're sure of. The Bateses are hard up. The funeral expenses were worrying Barry. Nick Felling says he carried full bottles of alcohol down to the cellar. The catering firm says he adjusted Diane's order and changed the arrangement to sale or return. Adrian says the back of the house that fewer people see isn't in such good nick as the front. Donna's diary says they argued about money and spending. The lists the two of them made of their stolen goods didn't match. That's not proof, but we can reasonably infer that things not out on display have been sold by Barry who was hoping Diane wouldn't miss them.' She paused for breath.

'You've been learning the file off by heart! What else can we reasonably infer?'

'That, until Tuesday afternoon, Barry was hoping that time, luck or Diane's inheritance would sort things out. And that he found out on Tuesday the terms of his father-in-law's will. Nick Felling said that it was after talking to Walter Denby that Barry had seemed off colour and went to sit in the conservatory. He'd be trying to pull himself together a bit before mixing with his guests again.'

Mitchell had been trying not to steal Jennifer's thunder, but he could stay silent no longer. 'There's a report from Shakila, an interview – not sanctioned by me – with a chap at Grant's place called Hallesby. He said Barry tinkered with cars and was on the list of people who had keys to the firm's garage.'

'Where would we be without Shakila?'

'We used to manage before she arrived.'

'Yes, but you weren't a high and mighty DCI in those days. You used to do all the daft things she gets into trouble for now.'

'We should have sent her to grill Bates. Do you realize that no one has? We've spoken to him of course, but only as a witness. He could have been in the spare bedroom any time he wanted. He could even have locked himself in with Lorraine while he was doing the deed. If anyone had tried the door they'd only have thought she'd locked it herself.' He reached for a chart from the file and studied it for several seconds. 'His print on the bedhead's in a position you'd need to steady yourself if you were left-handed.'

'Is he?'

Mitchell shrugged. 'We shall soon see.'

'He could have been in that position to do much pleasanter things to his wife.'

'What, in the spare room on a single bed?'

With a perfectly straight face, Jennifer told him, 'Not everyone's as straitlaced as you.'

Chapter Thirteen

The Mitchell children had rejoiced to have their father with them for the whole of Sunday. Mitchell himself had had more physical exercise since they woke that morning than in the whole of his week at work. They had all swum in the morning and flown kites in the park from lunch until dark. Then it had turned chilly and now they were gathered round a coal fire in their sitting room, eating tea there to celebrate this rare day spent together.

He surveyed his family with satisfaction. The four small individuals had few physical features in common – in fact, he and Ginny had been asked on a couple of occasions if their children had been adopted. Somehow, between them, he and Ginny had produced dark-haired, dreamy-eyed Declan. Caitlin had inherited his own blunt, uncompromising features, but was saved by her mother's slight build and grace of movement. Even the twins were not like each other. Sinead was a quicksilver child, dark-haired and blue-eyed, a Celt, while Michael at five was fat and fair. Nor did any of the four resemble any other in temperament.

Now, in the intervals of putting away hot sausage rolls, they were again engaged in a serious discussion. This topic had arisen from the fact that their happy day was their father's reward for putting yet another villain under lock and key. There seemed to be a general consensus that too much fuss was made about the problems of achieving peace and justice and instilling right values into all citizens.

Michael's solution was the simplest. 'It would be a better

world,' he announced, 'if we had flowers everywhere, like in the park. People should have them in gardens and pots and baskets.' He grew more fanciful. 'They should paint flowers on the roof and the walls and in all the places where flowers won't grow.'

And be accused of vandalism, Mitchell thought peevishly.

'No one,' Sinead added, 'should be allowed to burn houses down. My friend found a lighter, but luckily it broke.' Mitchell made a mental note to identify the friend and to check out his or her arsonist tendencies.

Caitlin chipped in on her usual practical level. 'The world would be better if there were no dog turds in our snicket.' Good old Kat! Down to basics as always. She had a carefully thought-out suggestion, though it seemed not to help much with the recalcitrant dogs. 'It might make everyone good if an important man in the government photocopied thousands of letters and sent them round, warning the bad people. They'd have to go to prison for a year if they took no notice. And . . .' She paused to eye Sinead sternly, perhaps as a warning against being influenced by her friend with the damaged lighter. '. . . we could control big fires by having robots that sense heat and then make foam come out of big long hoses.'

So Kat, having replaced the police with one letter-writing government officer, now proposed to make the fire service redundant with robots. Splendid! That should make the prospect of a few more days off a distinct possibility.

Declan, at ten, was not impressed with these impractical suggestions. 'It's not,' he announced loftily, 'as simple as that!'

Refreshed by his Sunday at home, Mitchell sat at his desk in his office on Monday morning, determined to complete the paperwork relating to Barry Bates's offences as quickly as he could. The weather was chilly and damp, the excitement of the chase was over. He gritted his teeth, turned his radiator on to its lowest setting and began the hated task.

From time to time he came up for breath and smiled to himself as he remembered the simplistic views of his offspring that had entertained him the evening before. Inevitably, because of the nature of his work, they had become aware of the darker side of life unnaturally early. It was healthy as well as amusing that they should, at their own level, have found solutions to the problems they heard about.

It occurred to him that most of the people of Cloughton who discussed the crimes and punishment of Barry Bates would take very much the same view of them as his children. This dangerous man had got his just deserts – though some would consider any sentence he was given too lenient.

By six o'clock, Mitchell was leaving the station with the satisfaction of having achieved what he had determined to do. The cold drizzle had given place to an almost clear sky with a mellow sun which hung low and shone cheerfully if not very warmly. The reward for his industrious day was given promptly. Virginia's brother, together with his new fiancée, had called to receive congratulations and had remained to offer their services as baby sitters for the evening.

Mitchell offered felicitations and thanks. 'I expect you want to know what you're letting yourselves in for. You're welcome to practise on our tribe any time you like.'

Charlotte displayed her hoop of sapphires and grinned at him. 'If ours behave as well as yours always do, we've no fears, though I think we'll stop before we've collected four.'

'Difficult when they start arriving in pairs.' Mitchell admired the ring, fetched Alex a bottle of Amarone from the cellar and raised an eyebrow at his wife. 'I suppose you've got the evening planned for us?'

Virginia nodded, named the pub restaurant where she had provisionally booked a table for herself and Benny and warned Charlotte about both her daughters' bizarre plans for bridesmaids' dresses and Declan's refusal to have any part in the bridal procession. 'Though he might be talked round to being an usher by the time it happens.' She noticed an exchange of glances between their visitors and smiled to herself.

In view of the improvement in the weather, and her husband's early arrival home, Virginia suggested that they should walk to the other side of town where their chosen pub stood at the foot of the abrupt tilt of land on the north side. 'Alex says he'll fetch us back when we ring him, so it won't matter if it rains.' Mitchell's spirits rose still further. Walking across the centre of Cloughton from their house provided everything they could see with a moorland background of hazy purples, greens and browns. Its soothing effect was emphasized rather than spoilt by the foreground of buildings, huddled under a smoky haze from which rose a couple of church spires, more mill chimneys and at least one pylon. The chimneys no longer belched smoke, most of the well-built and not unattractive mill buildings having been converted to purposes other than their original ones. Once they had made the turning at the end of their own street, the three aggressively thrusting tower blocks, which housed most of Cloughton's petty villains and which, in Mitchell's opinion, were the town's only eyesore, were all behind them.

Inevitably, the conversation revolved around Michell's current case. He needed to talk it out of his system and Virginia wanted to hear how it had all turned out. Her first question was not what Mitchell was expecting. 'Are the Grants suing you?'

Mitchell blinked. 'For wrongful arrest, you mean? No, but he says they considered it.'

'And decided, for the sake of the rest of the family, no doubt, their privacy and so on, to relinquish this opportunity to get even richer?'

Mitchell nodded. 'They claim all that – well, he does, anyway – but too many facts would come out about all Victor's liaisons. Really, they're more concerned than any of the others about keeping a low profile. Apparently, the wedding, Antonia's to Philip, is still on, so no one wants the papers full of Smith-Conroy or Bates-Grant scandals.'

'So, what was the clinching evidence against Barry Bates?'

'The simplest, thank goodness – a confession. He caved in more or less as soon as we challenged him. Like many one-off killers, Bates isn't a dyed-in-the-wool criminal. He can't avoid all the consequences of what he's done but he wants to sort out as much as possible and shield Diane in every way he can. Pleading guilty takes all the drama out of the proceedings.'

The roadway they were walking over was made of flags and setts. The buildings, with three storeys above ground level and cellar-dwellings below, revealed a way of life that had vanished and they were now the backs of well-fitted-out shops that fronted a main street. They paused to admire afresh the long row with its outside landings bounded by well-maintained wrought iron rails, though neither of them commented.

Instead, Mitchell said, 'Diane Bates calmly announced that she would go to prison with her husband.'

'Why? Did she mean to be taken seriously?'

Mitchell shrugged. 'She hadn't thought that far herself. I think she has a vague idea of damp dungeons for low-class riff-raff and druggies, and suitable accommodation for middle-class people who have only committed white collar crimes.'

'Like suffocating your sister-in-law?'

'She says that was done under stress and in panic and wasn't typical behaviour for Barry.'

'She's very likely right. That hardly excuses him. Even serial killers don't dispose of their victims once a week. Their sprees are aberrations in seemingly normal behaviour or it wouldn't give you so much trouble to hunt them out.'

Virginia began walking again. Abstractedly, Mitchell wandered after her. 'She says Barry was furiously angry when he heard about Edgar Smith's will . . .'

'So he rushed upstairs and killed his daughter?'

'He blamed Lorraine for being his favourite, for playing up to him and cutting Diane out. He's tried to give her everything she wanted to compensate, until he got into serious difficulties and the tremendous amount of funeral expenses were the final straw. Diane's really beating herself up because she thinks the whole business started with her extravagance.'

'So she should. It did.'

'But Edgar's treatment made Diane as she is, and who knows what happened to Edgar Smith to make him obsess on just one daughter?'

Virginia sighed. She had spent a normal busy day, attending to the demands of four youngsters, writing a tricky article for a magazine and restoring reasonable order in a house full of toys, books and general family clutter. After the bleakness of the day, this unexpectedly lovely evening was just beginning to draw in. The curious yellowish light was lending an exotic quality even to the council houses at the bottom of the hill. Chimney pots, trees, concrete lampstands and telegraph poles were forming an elaborate tracery against the sky where luminous daylight was doing battle with the glow of burning sodium. Each made the other seem irrelevant and the combination gave a sensation of unreality. She wanted to drink it in and enjoy it.

However, Benny's questions needed an answer. She tuned in to him again.

'. . . she claims she's jointly responsible. If she hadn't thrown his money around he wouldn't have been driven to "borrow" Edgar's. And that in itself she didn't see as a serious crime. He expected to be able to put things right, either by clever speculation or when Edgar died and half the money came to them. The Smiths trusted him and would have accepted that a lot of the money was unavailable because it was tied up in long-term investments.'

'From what I've heard of Edgar, he was shrewder than that.'

'Maybe he was. I'm only telling you what the Bateses told me.'

200

'How long do you think they'll give him?'

'Who knows? Nick Felling seems prepared to take responsibility for Diane, which is pretty public-spirited after the way she's treated him.'

They had reached the last stage of their walk, through a corner of the People's Park. Virginia stopped by a bench in front of a bed of russet dahlias, most of them past their best but attractive in their shaggy outline. She knew their untidiness would irritate him and wished she had chosen another perch. He sat down beside her.

'You seem uneasy about this. You don't think you've got it wrong? Are you worried that he's covering for her?'

Mitchell shook his head unhesitatingly. 'No. I think, if she'd done it, she'd not let him take the blame. Her saving grace is that she does realize he's the one person who is uncompromisingly on her side. She wouldn't risk losing that.'

'So, what's your problem? You like nicking people, as you frequently tell us, and that's what you've done.'

'The problem is that there's always something to be said on the villain's side. He's usually been sinned against himself.'

'But Bates has had an easy life, cushy job, the best of everything.'

'Financially, yes, but I wouldn't think being married to Diane was very easy. I believed him when he said he'd do anything to make her happy. I honestly think he's more sorry because he's got her involved in this mess than because he's on trial for murder and attempted murder. He says he didn't intend to kill Donna.'

'I see, just put her into a state where she needed constant care from a mother substitute who wanted control of her and of her money. Very thoughtful of them.'

'It sounds mad, I know – or obsessed.'

'Isn't that the same thing? You're not God, Benny.'

'No, but Barry Bates is going to spend most if not all of the rest of his life in prison, taking the full rap for Lorraine Conroy's death. But Lorraine died because of Edgar's stupid parenting, because of her own selfish irresponsibility and because of his damaged wife's greed and snobbery.'

Virginia was losing patience. 'No, he isn't. He's going to pay for picking up a pillow and pushing it down on someone's face until she stopped breathing. That's what you'd have been saying to me before you got into this funny mood. There might be something to be said for your defence of him if he'd hit her in a temper, even stabbed her like the poor demented old chap who attacked Caroline. Barry Bates stood over his sister-in-law for several minutes, waiting for her to choke to death.

'By all means, stop thinking that nicking people is the be-all and end-all of your career if you like. Stick to being a policeman though. You aren't the raw material to make a social worker.'

He smiled at her. 'Maybe that's good advice. The police are paid more and we've got four children to keep. I'm just getting old. I'm nearly forty, you wouldn't understand that!'

She got up and stalked off down the path, then stopped to call back to him. 'I understand arithmetic though. You've got another seven per cent of your current life span to live before you're forty. Now, you can please yourself but I'm off to the pub. I'm hungry!'

Epilogue

For Mitchell and his family, the end of his case had changed their life to a large degree, at least until the next violent death. For the rest of the people of Cloughton, it made little impact beyond spicing their conversations when the *Clarion* released a wealth of personal details about the victims and the perpetrator on the following Wednesday.

Ray Holland, for instance, in another laboratory in another town in his designated area of authority, was offering the same demonstration of his skill combined with the same recital of startling historical facts in his chosen field of study. 'Do you know,' he demanded, his glittering spectacles and erect hair turned with severity on his latest first-timer, 'that in the Museum of Alexandria there are accounts from the third and fourth centuries BC which describe not only autopsies, but live dissection of criminals.'

He paused to concentrate on a particularly ticklish bit of dissection of his own before cheerfully continuing the education of his audience. He had moved on by several millennia, and back to Britain. '. . . a Kentish manuscript, the September Articles, written in 1194. In those days, coroners were always on the lookout for signs of suicide. It was a crime against God and the King and the punishment was to forfeit the offender's estate – a very handy source of royal income. It meant destitution for the corpse's relatives but rich pickings for an obliging coroner who could please the King by "finding suitable evidence".'

Dr Holland was a little disappointed to find his current

first-timer was made of strong stuff. The young man remained in the lab and accepted, quite phlegmatically, both types of instruction he was being offered.

Miriam Scott was buried as quietly as she had died. After the simple ceremony, her husband's palatial house, acquired before his wife's illness began, was put up for sale. He intended to donate the proceeds to his research project into Addison's disease. Having resigned his hospital post before he could be dismissed from it, he was not, of course, allowed to direct its work actively. However, he remained free to watch its progress and to finance it, since not one person who had formerly co-operated in his experiments could be persuaded to make a charge against him.

Antonia Grant decided, in the end, that she would remain engaged to be married to Philip Conroy. She would suggest that they schedule the wedding for sometime towards the end of next summer. By then, the family scandal should have died down as far as it ever was going to.

She didn't want to leave it any longer than was necessary. She was already thirty-two, nine years older than Philip. She knew that she was not really a career woman. Resentfully, she remembered overhearing Lorraine Conroy's advice to her son. 'Find someone else, Philip. That one hasn't got the nous to make a Yorkshire pudding, never mind help you with the running of Vic's firm.' She would love to feel that this opinion was unjustified but she was honest enough with herself, if not with others, to know that her apparent successes with clients were masterminded by her father, who expected that Philip would continue to protect her.

The hurry to marry was, of course, nothing to do with the possibility of their having children. That was not on the agenda. What she must avoid was any suggestion, especially from the press, that she was on the shelf. It was a bit late to look elsewhere now, and at least she had been relieved of the risk of having to get rid of Lorraine.

Debbie Collins and her friend Shaun received not a few odd glances as they progressed, one reluctant, one fired with enthusiasm, along Elm Road. They passed number 8, the Bateses' former home. The address meant nothing to Shaun, and Debbie made no comment on the For Sale sign in the front garden.

Panting alarmingly between words, Debbie complained, 'You never said nothing about carrying on with this in the bloody rain!'

Shaun advised her to save her breath for moving herself. Since he had 'obliged' DC Clement by agreeing to wear a pair of his plum-coloured tracksters that had 'become too baggy' for him, Shaun had donated his jogging pants to Debbie. That resourceful young woman, after pausing to check, 'You aren't going to whinge for 'em back?' had cut the legs down to her own size and threaded string into the waistband. He had promised to give her her own pair of tracksters for Christmas.

She was unimpressed by his generosity. 'Aye, if you find any more hanging on that copper's line!'

At the next junction they paused for Debbie to catch her breath. Shaun tried to curb his impatience at this break in his rhythmic stride. When she was capable of speech again, she warned him, 'I don't know how much longer I'm going to carry on with this lark.' She suspected that she might be pregnant. She was not overly concerned about her condition. Her own mother had conceived her when she was only one year older and had raised her with very little help. That had turned out well enough. She might even find that Shaun decided to take an interest. At the very least it might soon let her off the hook over this stupid running business.

Long before Debbie considered herself fully recovered, Shaun had set off again. 'Come on, Debs. Another half mile and we'll stop for a cuddle in the churchyard.'

When they reached it, however, Debbie was denied her reward. A procession of three limousines was approaching the church. Through the window of the first, Debbie saw a familiar face. 'God, this is Donna's mum's funeral! Let go of me, you plonker, and show a bit of respect.'

In spite of her authoritative command she had expected to be ignored. She was surprised and touched when, as the procession passed them, Shaun reluctantly removed his Leeds United woolly cap. From the first car, Diane Bates glared at them indignantly, but Nicholas Felling managed a grateful smile.

Donna Felling walked round the dining room in their house in Maybridge with only a slight limp, which, her doctors assured her, would gradually disappear. She was proud of the final result of her work of the last two days. The table was covered with a crisp white cloth into which she had ironed no creases. Not all the cutlery matched exactly. Dad wasn't fussy about things like that. The new napkins he'd let her buy, though, were beautiful and the flowers she had picked from the garden were better than any she had seen in a shop – the last of the dahlias, a late flower from the hibiscus that had opened only that morning and some strands of ivy that trailed from the vase. 'Very artistic,' Dad had said.

She couldn't understand why Dad and Auntie Diane were surprised to find she was such a good cook. Who did they think had prepared all the meals when she had lived here with Mum? She had done most of the cooking earlier. The beef casserole that she had prepared yesterday had been simmering in the oven now for two and a half hours. The pudding was sitting in the fridge. You couldn't go wrong with cheesecake and this recipe had only needed mixing – no cooking. Only the first course was a bit risky but she would rise to the challenge.

Dad had said that organizing a housewarming party would be too much for her. She had argued that, until she was allowed back to school after Christmas, she hadn't very much to do except read.

She loved reading, of course, but you couldn't do it all day, every day. Anyway, her consultant had said she was to take moderate exercise. She defied Dad to prove that standing at the kitchen table and walking to the oven was more than moderate, and he had taken her in the Yellow Peril to do the food shopping. She was glad they'd kept it. A new car wouldn't be half as much fun, though it was good to know they could afford to have it mended when it wouldn't go.

She didn't think she wanted to be rich, but that was just as well because she suspected Dad was going to give half the money away. She knew for a fact that he'd put a lot into Uncle Barry's bank to sort out some trouble there for Auntie Diane. He was helping her to sell her big house and buy a smaller one, and they actually seemed to like each other now, most of the time, anyway.

When she realized that her aunt was poorer than she used to be, Donna had wondered whether she ought to give back the lily-of-the-valley egg, which Auntie Diane had given her as a Get Well present when she was still in hospital. But apparently it wasn't really very valuable after all, and Dad had said it would be all right for Donna to keep it. He was going to sort something out for her aunt when the lawyers had finished all their complicated business.

The doorbell rang and Donna wondered which of their eight guests it was who was first to arrive. Dad would sort out whoever it was. Donna had a soufflé to worry about.